Simon Grave

and the
Wrath of
Grapes

Len Boswell

Black Rose Writing | Texas

First printing

This is a work of fiction. Names, characters, businesses, places, events, and incidents are either the products of the author's imagination or used in a fictitious manner. Any resemblance to actual persons, living or dead, or actual events is purely coincidental.

ISBN: 978-1-68513-154-8
PUBLISHED BY BLACK ROSE WRITING
www.blackrosewriting.com

Printed in the United States of America
Suggested Retail Price (SRP) $20.95

Simon Grave and the Wrath of Grapes is printed in Palatino Linotype

*As a planet-friendly publisher, Black Rose Writing does its best to eliminate unnecessary waste to reduce paper usage and energy costs, while never compromising the reading experience. As a result, the final word count vs. page count may not meet common expectations.

To all I love without condition
To all I love without omission

Never doubt

And to Shadow, my beloved Weimaraner, who could snatch birds out of the sky just like that, and who could run with the grace and power of a stallion. Good boy!

Other books by
Len Boswell

Simon Grave Mysteries:
A Grave Misunderstanding
Simon Grave and the Curious Incident of the Cat in the Daytime
Simon Grave and the Drone of the Basque Orvilles
Simon Grave and the Sons of Irony
Simon Grave and the School of Casual Invisibility

Other Mysteries:
Flicker: A Paranormal Mystery
Skeleton: A Bare Bones Mystery

Memoirs:
Santa Takes a Tumble
Unboxing Raymond

Nonfiction:
The Leadership Secrets of Squirrels
Stick Figures: The Life and Art of Len Boswell

Fantasies:
The Cave of the Six Arrows
The Fool's Gambit
Barnum's Angel

Simon Grave
and the
Wrath of Grapes

"It is the wine that leads me on, the wild wine that sets the wisest man to sing at the top of his lungs, laugh like a fool—it drives the man to dancing... it even tempts him to blurt out stories better never told."

—Homer, *The Odyssey*

"As I ate the oysters with their strong taste of the sea and their faint metallic taste that the cold white wine washed away, leaving only the sea taste and the succulent texture, and as I drank their cold liquid from each shell and washed it down with the crisp taste of the wine, I lost the empty feeling and began to be happy and to make plans."

—Ernest Hemingway, *A Moveable Feast*

"We are all mortal until the first kiss and the second glass of wine."

—Eduardo Galeano

1

In the beginning, there was something in the nothing and everything in the something. A highly compact little mass, dense as all get-out and containing nothing less than the future, came from seemingly out of nowhere to sit poised and alert in the nothingness, waiting for something to happen in a place it found convenient to wait.

It waited, and waited, but nothing happened in the nothingness.

Then the profound density, which now called itself the Universe, began to feel queasier and queasier. In the end before the beginning, it barely had time to get out a weak "uh-oh" before it exploded in what scientists today call the Big Bang, the little dense mass becoming untold bigger things, all hurtling outward in every direction at great speed.

The Eon of Pinball Chaos followed, invisible flippers, which some say were operated by a god and others by a lunatic, sending the pieces yon and hither, the sound of bells ringing throughout a universe without ears. Then came the Eon of Random Decisions, some matter deciding to become stars, other matter condensing into planets, and still other matter forming matter-gobbling black holes, while all the rest, the rebel matter, felt a need, the need for speed, and decided to stay with the thrill of hurtling through space.

The Eon of Not Much Going On came next, stars growing brighter and collecting planets, planets growing cooler and collecting moons, and moons taking it on the chin as rebel matter, directionless and not that bright, crashed into them. It was fun at first—so many collisions!—but the Universe soon became bored. "Is this all there is?" was its common refrain.

Some say that what happened next, the Eon of Holy Shit, I Didn't See that Coming, was the work of rebel matter, while others insist that the Flipper God was responsible. In any event, or actually in many events, something called life oozed, slithered, swam, crawled, walked, ran, and flew into existence in various forms, some elegant in aspect and others, e.g., hovercraft salesmen, hideous to behold and best avoided at all costs.

But the Universe, which appreciated a good joke, couldn't help chuckling. This could get interesting, it thought. And so it settled down and watched.

Simon Grave woke with a start. He had been having a wonderful dream about a female gymnast when the dream was interrupted by the approach of a dense, dark mass that seemed to hover over him, chuckling. His bedroom at the top of the lighthouse was dark, the Surround Vision playing a public television broadcast of a trip to Mars. His bed seemed to be floating in the nothingness as the Mars Colony Transport Vehicle glided by, an image of Mars growing larger and larger.

"Stop!" he shouted.

Mars, the spaceship, and the looming darkness disappeared, the window curtains opening automatically, sun streaming in to light up the room.

Grave shielded his eyes and buried his face in a pillow. "Not so frickin' bright," he said, and the curtains stopped and modulated the incoming light. He peeked out from the pillow. "That's better."

He rolled across the bed and sat up, rubbing at his eyes and stretching. "Time, please."

A visual display of the time—9:46 a.m.—popped up on the far wall. "Yikes!"

He scrambled to his feet and ran to the closet. He was late, or at least would be late if he didn't get dressed quickly.

It was a rare day off, so he ignored the five gray suits hanging neatly in the closet, as well as a similar number of the Hawaiian shirts and white cotton slacks he favored on his days off. But not this day. No, he had bought something special for this day, his first official date with Detective Polly Loblolly.

"Where is it?" He began to panic. The package with the new outfit had arrived only yesterday via Drone Freight Services, and he was sure he had put it in the closet.

And then there it was, leaning up against the back wall of the closet. "Ah."

He pulled out the package, dropped it on the bed, and ripped it open. "What the—"

He had ordered a pair of khakis and a brown and white checked shirt, but neither item was in evidence.

He pulled out a pair of pants and a shirt. Both were mirror-finished and shone brightly in the sunlight. The tag on both identified the items as ScreenWear, a new line of clothing featuring multiple looks. "One price, many looks" was printed just below the logo.

He shook them out and looked at them. They seemed to be the right size, but could he wear them? They were a new trend, so Polly would probably like the idea that he was being uncharacteristically adventurous.

"Let's see," he said, tugging on the slacks. "Not too bad." He searched in the packaging. "Now how do I make them work?"

A little instruction book popped out of the box when he shook it. All he had to do, it said, was press one or more of a series of buttons on the built-in belt to change the color or pattern of the material.

He tried pushing the first button, and the slacks turned from a mirror finish to a dull gray. When he pressed the second button, various patterns appeared in the gray: check, herringbone, little pigs, big dragons, and variations of tie-dyed cloth. "Humph."

He pushed the third button and the patterns themselves changed colors, some working well with the gray background and others not. "Humph."

He pushed the fourth button and the patterns began to move and swirl. "Whoa, don't need that."

He pushed the fourth button again and the patterns stopped moving. "Better."

He looked at the fifth and last button, wondering what it might do. He gave it a little push and images from a movie began to appear on the slacks. There seemed to be a car chase taking place on the slacks, the cars weaving around the legs and the waist.

He pushed the fifth button again, hoping to stop the action, but the second push only turned on the sound of the roaring engines.

He quickly pushed the fifth button again, and the slacks returned to their original mirrored finish. He nodded to himself. *Stick with the first two buttons*, he thought.

He tugged on the pants and adjusted the colors to plain gray. Then he donned the shirt, which had a similar series of buttons. He adjusted the color to a pale yellow, added a check pattern, and turned the check to a medium brown.

He glanced at the clock. 10:02. He would just have enough time to grab a cup of coffee. He spotted his shoes near the bed, tugged them on, and headed down the circular stair to the next level, which served as a kitchen.

His manservant, Roderick, who was built to resemble the late actor Peter Lorre, was sitting at the table with Grave's guests: Red, the carcinologist, a simdroid built to resemble a steamed crab in every detail, including size, and Horace, a seagull with a neural node implant that provided him with humanlike intelligence and the ability to speak—and eat French fries.

Red was watching as Roderick fed Horace French fry after French fry.

"What are you doing?" said Grave.

"An experiment," said Red. "How many French fries can Horace here eat in a single sitting?"

Grave shook his head. "I think you'll find he's bottomless."

Horace squawked. "You got that right." He turned to Roderick. "I'll have another."

Roderick held up a fry and Horace snapped it out of his hand. "More salt, less vinegar," he said.

Roderick nodded. "I'll just make a slight adjustment in the synthesizer."

"Before you do that," said Grave. "How about some coffee? I'm running out of time."

"Ah, the date, sir?" said Roderick.

Grave shook his head. "It's not really a date."

"Not a date? You're taking her out aren't you?"

"No, I'm meeting her at the winery."

Roderick scoffed. "So not picking her up means it's not a date?"

"Yes, pretty much."

"Oh, sir, I think you'll find she has a different idea about this, um, meeting."

"Like what?"

"Oh, I'm sure she thinks it's a date."

Grave considered the idea. "You think?"

"Oh, indeed, sir."

Grave sighed. "Well, we'll see how it goes."

"Yes, sir."

"Now, about that coffee, and has anyone seen Barry?"

Horace flapped his wings. "Your annoying drone is downstairs. Calling a hovercab, I think." He turned to Roderick. "More fries!"

Roderick growled at him. "Don't ruffle your feathers. It will just be a moment. I have to get Simon a coffee."

Grave waved him off. "Never mind the coffee. It's a long drive to the winery, so I'd better get going."

"Winery?" said Horace. "What winery?"

Grave pointed to an empty wine bottle on the counter. "Château de Crabe Rouge, just like it says on the bottle."

Horace offered up a seagull version of a chuckle. "There's no such thing."

"Of course there is," said Grave. "It's in Crab Valley."

Horace chuckled again and gave Grave a look of disbelief. "Do you believe everything printed on a bottle? There's no such place."

"Of course there is."

"Oh, and you've been there?"

"No, but I'll be going there today, for a tour of the winery."

Horace shook his head. "Look, I've flown all over Crab Cove and the Greater Crabopolis, and I can say quite unequivocally, there's no such place. Not nowhere. Not no how."

"Well, it's not close by," said Grave. "That's why I have to be on my way. It's some distance from here, on or beyond the far outskirts of town. Barry knows where it is and I'm sure the hovercab will, too."

Horace shook his head. "Well, go then. You'll see I'm right."

Grave rolled his eyes. "Well, we'll see who sees, I guess."

"Indeed," said Horace.

Grave started to say something more, but then he just threw up his hands. No sense continuing this argument further. "All right, I'm out of here."

He turned and started down the stairs to the ground level. He could hear Horace behind him, begging for more French fries.

2

The moment he stepped into the hovercraft he regretted his decision not to take his vintage 1965 Austin Healey Sprite instead. The Sprite and its nonstop, full-volume gospel music would have calmed him down, made him less nervous about his date—was it really a date?—with Polly.

Now he not only had to worry about Polly, but he had to worry about placing his life in the virtual hands of a driverless vehicle. Yes, they had a wonderful safety record, but still, it only took one little mistake in code to see him and the hovercab splattered against a wall.

Barry, who usually flew alongside cabs, seemed to sense Grave's apprehension and opted to ride inside with him.

"Don't worry. Everything will be fine," Barry said.

Grave nodded, but it was the quick nod of a nervous person.

"Seriously, sir, it will be fine. You'll be fine. She'll be fine. We'll be fine. The whole wide world will be fine."

Grave sighed. "Horace doesn't think Crab Valley exists."

Barry said nothing.

"I said—"

"I heard you. The thing is, he's right in a sense."

"In a sense? What do you mean?"

"This whole Crab Valley thing on the bottle."

"And?"

"Seems it's just a marketing ploy."

"Wait, are you saying there's no Crab Valley? Then where are we going?"

"Oh, we're going there, but it's not like you imagine."

"How do you know what I imagine?"

"How? You've been talking about it pretty much nonstop since you decided to take the tour. You're expecting rolling hills and rows and rows of grape vines heavy with grapes. You're expecting young maidens mashing the grapes with their feet. You're expecting a bucolic scene with happy dogs and sleepy cats. You're expecting—"

"Okay, okay, and why is that wrong?"

"You'll see."

"No, tell me."

Barry lifted off the seat and rotated to look out the window. "No, we're here. You'll see."

Grave was incredulous. "Here? How could we be here already? Looks like some kind of industrial park."

"That's because it is. Check out the sign."

Grave strained his neck to get a look at the sign they were approaching: Crab Valley Industrial Park. "What the—"

The hovercab slowed and turned left into the industrial park. Grave could see Polly pacing back and forth outside a low, rectangular, architecture-free building as gray as death, a weather-worn sign across the entrance announcing, "Château de Crabe Rouge." Her new drone, Sparky, a mirrored drone the size of a fist, sparkled just above her head in the morning light. When Loblolly spotted him, she threw up her arms as if to say, "What the—"

Grave groaned.

3

Grave was slow in leaving the hovercab, for two reasons. First, he knew his attempt at a date had already been destroyed. Whatever lay within that concrete slab of a building would never restore his image of what a winery should be, so why rush it? Besides, he could see the disappointment—even anger—in Loblolly's face. And second, he had never seen her look lovelier, and he wanted a moment to take her in.

Like Grave, she had made an effort to wear something out of the ordinary, something she would never wear to work. The red dress was barely a dress at all. It looked like a shiny red leather tube that she had somehow slithered into. But to Grave, the startling thing was not the dress, but Loblolly herself.

Detective Loblolly was tall and shapely, with legs from here to Boise and back again. She checked every box for his dream woman. Eyes, sky blue. Nose, turned up. Skin, a golden tan. Lips, full and pouty. Hair, honey blond and long. Body, toned. Breasts, abundant. Smile, disarming. Neck, long and almost regal.

There's beauty and there's beauty. Some women are an acquired taste; their beauty comes at you in subtle changes in mood and expression, the way they tilt their heads when they speak or run their hands through their hair. It's a nuanced beauty, one you grow to appreciate, often deeply, over time.

Loblolly's beauty came at you like a coast-to-coast gravity train you couldn't avoid. You could only startle, jump back, and wonder at its approach. Not that you'd ever find Loblolly's face on a magazine cover. Hers was a girl-next-door beauty, almost tomboyish, but still powerful and undeniable. And it came with the deep, lusty voice of a blues singer.

But when he thought about her, beauty was not the major attraction. It was more like a bonus thrown in at the last minute to sweeten the deal. But the deal was her intelligence, self-confidence, and sense of humor. He simply delighted in just being around her.

Loblolly walked up to the hovercab and rapped her knuckles on the window. "Are you getting out, or what?"

Grave sighed, gave her a nod, and opened the door. Getting out was another matter. His new trousers were a little tight, so when he bent over to get out, he inadvertently activated a series of buttons that made his pants strobe with red and black polka dots.

4

Detective Polly Loblolly couldn't help smiling as she watched Grave dancing beside the hovercab, slapping at his pants. The polka dots changed to red and yellow and then were replaced by an evolving scene from a war movie, machine gun fire streaming up his shirt as explosions hit both his knees.

And still he slapped and danced.

Loblolly wondered what she had ever seen in this almost handsome man, but in truth, she knew she was hooked. She liked his tall frame and square jaw. Her friend Detective Snoot said he reminded her of Dudley Do-Right, a cartoon character from long ago, a character that featured just such a physical frame and a personality, like Grave's, that tended toward a woeful but nevertheless charming naïveté. She thought about that. No, he *was* like Dudley Do-Right all right, but with a soupçon of Sherlock Holmes thrown in. He may be a little strange, but he was a fine detective.

His eyes were blue in the way that glaciers were blue, and gray in a way that clouds were gray before a storm. His nose was strong and prominent, with a little speed bump in the middle. He had lips, of course, and they moved more or less as lips should do when he talked, but there was not much to say about them. His hair was something else entirely: thick and black and glistening from the combined effects of shampoos and conditioners faithfully applied each morning and topped with just enough gel to hold it in place.

Polly watched Simon for a few more seconds and then stepped forward, grabbed him by the belt, and tugged him to a stop. "Be still."

She pushed a sequence of buttons, and the trousers changed back to gray, along with the shirt. Now he looked like a just-released prisoner, but at least he wasn't strobing.

Grave looked down at his trousers. "How did you do that?"

She shrugged. "I have a pair of those. You just have to know the right sequence to push. It's one-four-three-two."

"Oh." He smiled at her. "Wonderful."

"Well, maybe," she said, pointing at the building. "This is not the winery you promised me."

"Nor the one I expected."

Grave looked around again to see if there was anything remotely *vineyardy* to be seen. There were a few hovercars parked at the far end of the parking lot, which seemed to be reserved for employees, and one man, a protestor of some sort, pacing back and forth in front of the entrance. He held a sign that shouted *SAVE THE GRAPES!*

"So, do we go in or call it a day?"

She chuckled. "Oh, you're not going to get rid of me that easily. Yes, we go in. I can't think of a better adventure." She looped her arm around Simon's and tugged him forward. "Come on, let's go in."

Grave turned to Barry. "Stay here."

"But—"

"No, seriously, get to know Sparky while we're inside."

"Yes," added Loblolly. "We don't want to be disturbed."

"Very well," said Barry, moving to hover beside Sparky. "We'll manage."

Sparky, whose voice mimicked Loblolly's—a new drone feature growing in popularity—moved an inch closer to Barry. "Yes, we'll be fine. You guys go on in."

Barry and Sparky watched in silence as Grave and Loblolly walked up to the door, opened it, and disappeared inside.

Barry waited until the door clicked shut and then turned to Sparky. "Do you think this is going to work?"

Sparky twirled in the air. "Not a chance in Hell."

Barry nodded. "The pants, right?"

Sparky chuckled. "For starters."

5

The interior of the Château de Crabe Rouge's building looked more like a chemical factory than a vineyard. Stainless steel piping ran along the walls and ceiling. Some of it seemed to connect to six large containment vessels at the center of the vast space, and some of it seemed to race away to infinity.

Grave and Loblolly stood there, trying to make sense of what they were seeing.

"Where are the grapes?" said Grave.

"The containers, maybe?" said Loblolly, not at all sure.

A voice approaching them from behind tried to help. "Welcome to the processing and fermentation facility of Château de Crabe Rouge, synthesizers of fine simwines since 2037. By chance, are you here for a tour?"

Grave and Loblolly turned at the sound of the voice and then tried not to laugh. The voice was coming from a simdroid with grapes piled on top of his head. He was taller than Grave by more than a foot, and equally wider, giving him an aspect not only of robust health, but of something more godlike. His eyes danced, his smile sparkled, and his laugh resounded throughout the building as if it was amplified somehow. He wore what looked like a toga of some kind, but one that barely covered him. He carried a staff topped by a pine cone, which he swung to and fro as he spoke.

"Yes," said Grave. "We're here for the tour."

"Welcome to you both. My name is Bacchus, and I will be your guide for this informative tour of the facility."

Loblolly smiled up at him. "Bacchus? As in the Roman god Bacchus, god of wine?"

"Yes," said Bacchus, "and of farming and fertility. Son of Jupiter, etcetera, etcetera, at your service."

"Wonderful," said Loblolly. "Where do we begin?"

Bacchus tapped his staff on the concrete floor three times. "We begin at the beginning, of course." He pointed to a spot a few feet away. "See that red X on the floor? That's where we start."

"Good," said Grave. "So, we were just wondering where you keep the grapes."

Bacchus's deep laugh echoed throughout the facility. "Grapes, there are no grapes. We *synthesize* wine here. Thirty-seven chemicals and an assortment of nanobots conspire to create wines like no others—and certainly better than wines created from grapes." He gave them a sour look to indicate his disgust for real grapes. "Now, let us to the mark."

He strode across the floor to the X and beckoned them to join him. "Here, we begin here. Come, come, hurry now."

Grave and Loblolly scooted over next to him.

"Good," said Bacchus. "Now, should I begin with the history of wine-making and the impact of climate change on the industry or should we just get on with it, look at the facility—how we do what we do—and then end with a bottomless glass or six of Duct Tape Chardonnay, the wine that can fix anything?"

Grave and Loblolly looked at each other, not sure which tour the other would like.

"I see you are indecisive. Don't worry, most people are. The topic can be overwhelming. Tell you what, you seem like smart folks. Let's do this. I'll show you the facility, and you can ask questions as we go along. How about that? Are you up for that approach?"

Grave and Loblolly nodded like small children in thrall of a magician. "Yes," they said simultaneously.

Bacchus laughed again and tapped his staff hard, once, on the floor. "Come then." He waved his staff in the air to take in the entire facility. "All this, this plumbing, these tanks, are the key to it all."

A question suddenly came to Grave's mind, one that he had wrestled with over the years. "A question, if you will?"

"Certainly," said Bacchus. "And what might that be?"

"Well," said Grave, "I've noticed over the years that each vintage is exactly the same. The taste doesn't vary."

Bacchus leaned over to come face to face with Grave, his thick black eyebrows waggling with delight. "A wonderful question!"

He pulled back from Grave's face and pointed at the large vessels. "Year after year, the same chemicals flow into and out of those tanks. Every second of that flow is monitored by scientists and engineers with one goal: to make each sip of our wine taste exactly the same, for eternity if we're lucky."

"I see," said Grave.

"Perhaps you do, but wait, there's more."

"Like what?"

"Think about it. Chemistry is as objective as can be. You mix them consistently, under the same conditions of temperature, pressure, and so on, and you get the same result."

"Yes," said Grave. "So . . ."

Bacchus waved him off. "So, consider taste. Taste isn't objective at all. It's as subjective as can be, and each of us has different tastes and abilities to taste."

"Yes, so . . ."

"So, that's bad for business."

Grave blinked. "Wait, what?"

Loblolly grabbed his arm. "I think what Bacchus is trying to say is that if they go to all this trouble to make the wine consistently the same from year to year, only to have some people like its taste and others hate it, well, that isn't good for business, is it?"

Bacchus laughed. "This beautiful young woman understands me perfectly."

Grave smiled at Loblolly, then turned back to Bacchus. "But that's just the nature of business, isn't it? I mean, you can't expect everyone to like your product."

Bacchus glowered at him. "Sir, there's an old saying. *You can lead a horse to water, but you can't make him drink.* Are you familiar with that?"

Grave shrugged. "Yes, of course, which I think was my point exactly."

Bacchus nodded. "It's a silly saying. Defeatist, if you ask me. If you're going to all that trouble to lead the horse to water, you damn well want him to drink and will do everything you can to make him drink."

"I guess," said Grave, not sure where Bacchus was going.

Bacchus scoffed. "You guess, you guess. Well, we don't *guess* here at the Château de Crabe Rouge. We make it so. For us, the saying is, you can lead a horse to wine, and you can make a jackass out of him through chemistry."

"That's an odd saying," said Grave.

Bacchus sighed. "I'm still working on it, as are we."

Grave threw up his hands. "I'm sorry, I'm afraid you've lost me with all this talk of horses."

Bacchus rolled his eyes. "Tourists. Okay, okay, let me get to the point."

"Please."

Bacchus thought for a moment, and then began. "When we make our wine, we want the wine to be consistent, yes?"

"Yes, of course."

"Good. Now, we also want each and every one of our customers to have the same tasting experience. We want you, sir, and you, madam, to taste exactly the same thing."

"Sounds like a pipedream," said Grave.

"Wait," said Loblolly. "I think our friend here is about to explain it to us."

"Indeed," said Bacchus. He motioned them to come closer, and then bent down and whispered, "Nanobots. Our wine is filled with nanobots, little critters on a mission."

Grave shook his head. "I think I was more comfortable with horses and jackasses. But okay, what about these nanobots?"

"The nanobots make your taste buds conform to our idea of taste. If your taste buds are not inclined to like our wine, our little nanobots go to work, changing their perception of the liquid flowing by them."

Loblolly's eyes grew wide. "That's ingenious!"

Bacchus chuckled. "It is, it is. And our market share reflects that. No one has our technology. No one. Soon we will be the only wine people like, and then it's game over."

Grave frowned. "Doesn't seem very sporting."

Bacchus cocked his head. "Sir, we're talking business, ruthless, cut-throat business, the thing that makes our country great."

Grave was about to embark on a soliloquy defending diversity in all things, including taste and the marketplace, and damning cut-throat capitalism, but a singular sound stopped him.

It was a scream. A scream best not ignored. If blood could actually curdle from a scream, this was the scream that would have done it.

6

Chief Medical Examiner Jeremy Polk walked clockwise around the body, paused to stroke his chin, and then walked counterclockwise around it.

"So, what do you think?" said Grave.

Polk ignored him, taking another clockwise spin around the body.

"Seriously," said Grave. "You must have some idea about cause of death."

Polk bristled, stretching his small frame as high as he could, affecting a posture that had earned him the nickname Little Napoleon. "Yes, of course, but still . . ."

Grave rolled his eyes. "Let me help you. We pulled this man from the fermentation tank over there. Look, you can see the trail of wine."

Polk held up a hand. "I know that, I know that. The question is whether he died from drowning or from the rather gaping wounds in his chest. Do we know who he is?"

Loblolly broke in. "Yes, he's Falcon Fontaine, owner-vintner of this winery."

"Humph," said Polk, adding a second "humph" for good measure. "Seems he got too close to his business, or someone didn't like him or his wine."

"So which is it, drowning or stabbing."

Polk chuckled sardonically. "I would have thought by now that you would know the answer immediately, Grave. I mean put on your thinking cap. Look at the color of the wine."

Grave turned and looked at the trail. "A fine rosé, no doubt."

Polk laughed. "Ha! More like a questionable chardonnay spoiled by blood."

"It's blood?"

"Indeed. Which means . . . ?"

"He was stabbed to death and then thrown into the tank."

"Precisely."

"But when?"

"That's a bit difficult. The wine and the cold would have had a preservative effect on the body. I'll have to get him back to the morgue and open him up before I can give you a reasonable time of death."

"What about an *unreasonable* time of death?"

Polk sighed. "Grave, you know I don't like to do that."

"But can you at least bracket it for us. That will help us get this investigation started."

Loblolly gave Polk her patented sexy smile. "Come on, Jeremy. Just a guess will do at this point."

Polk blushed and then smiled back at her. "Very well. I'd guess the murder took place within the past forty-eight hours."

Grave raised a hand, but Polk slapped it down. "And no, I can't be any more precise than that."

"Could it have been recently? I mean like in the last few minutes?"

Polk started to say no, but then stopped. "Just a second." He walked over to the fermentation tank and peered through the viewing port. "Hmm."

"Hmm, what?"

"The wine is now a uniform pink."

"So?"

"So the blood has had time to mix in with the wine. Its uniform color indicates the passage of time."

"How much time?"

Polk puffed out a sigh and looked at the ceiling, his eyebrows dancing as if he were in deep thought, calculating the time required for X amount of blood to disperse in Y amount of wine at Z temperature. "Have you heard of the Brownian Movement?"

"You mean the rock band?" said Loblolly.

Polk startled. "There is such a thing?"

"Yes," said Loblolly. "Very popular."

"Humph," said Polk. "Never heard of them, but that's not the point. Brownian Movement is—well, never mind about that, it's just a law of physics that suggests that over time the blood coming from the victim's wounds will spread evenly throughout the wine."

"Um, okay," said Loblolly. "And how long would that take, exactly? Or approximately?"

"I'd say at least six hours," said Polk. "I can give you a more precise time when I get back to my computer."

"All right," said Grave, "but let us know as soon as you do."

"Meanwhile," said Loblolly, "we'll bring the others up to speed and start interviewing possible suspects: family members, competitors, employees—you now, the usual."

Polk nodded and pointed toward the door. "And here come the others, just in time."

Grave turned, then motioned for the others to approach the body.

Captain Henry Morgan, Detective Charlize Holmes, Dr. Smithers-Watson, and Detective Amanda Snoot walked forward, their heads on swivels, taking in the innards of Château de Crabe Rouge.

7

Captain Henry Morgan was never a man to beat around the bush. "So what've we got, Polk?"

And neither was Polk. "Body. Man. Dead. Said to be the owner. Multiple stab wounds. Massive loss of blood. Dumped in the fermentation tank over there."

Morgan grunted, his go-to reaction to the receipt of information of all kinds. He had a nuanced repertoire of grunts, each serving a different purpose. The current grunt indicated that he had received and understood what had been said but still wanted more clarifying information.

Grunts suited this bald, fireplug of a man. No-necked and wide as he was tall, he was an imposing figure, even at rest. He had shark eyes, dark and black and lifeless, and a face that suggested an early career as a boxer. His nose, hardly more than a blob at the center of his face, sat above a caterpillar-like moustache that had gone gray years ago. He wore the traditional blue uniform of a chief of police, but you could tell by the deep crease marks that it was a uniform two sizes too small for him.

Polk, who had worked with Morgan many years, knew exactly what was required by Morgan's grunt. "Body discovered by an employee. Her scream alerted Grave and Loblolly, who of course violated rules and tugged the body out of the tank, disturbing the crime scene."

Morgan seemed to notice Grave and Loblolly for the first time. "Jesus, what are you guys all dressed up for?"

Loblolly looked down at the floor. "Well, um, you see—"

Grave jumped in. "Our day off. We thought we'd take a tour."

Morgan grunted. This grunt, which was longer and lower-pitched than the first one, indicated that Morgan knew they were leaving information out. "So," he said, "a date is it?"

Grave startled, his right hand inadvertently touching the buttons on his belt. Whatever the combination was, his pants and shirt were now showing images of squirrels chasing each other around the trunk of a tree.

Morgan grunted. Translation: "What the—"

8

Captain Morgan shook his head at Grave one last time, then turned back to the others. "Now that we have Grave's pants under control, let's talk about who does what."

"Wait a minute," said Grave. "Where's Sergeant Blunt?"

Morgan sighed. "Will you please not interrupt? Blunt's back at the station, studying for his lieutenant's exam."

"Oh, yeah, I forgot."

Morgan rolled his eyes. "I'm sure you did. Now, let's get on with this. Grave, you and Loblolly were first on the scene, so I'll let you take the lead, with her as your temporary partner."

"Great," said Grave. "We'll talk to the employees first."

Morgan held up a hand. "No, let me make myself a little clearer. You'll be in charge of the case once you get out of those pants and she gets out of that fire-engine red dress. Go home, both of you, and change. Then, since you're already out of the building, go to this Fontaine guy's home and break the news to his relatives. Got it?"

Grave and Loblolly nodded.

"All right, so who do you want to do what, Grave?"

Grave puffed out a deep breath. "Okay, Charlize and Smithers should take on the employee interviews. Snoot, you can help with that, too, but first I'd like you to interview a guy in the parking lot. A protestor of some sort."

Snoot nodded. "I saw him. Okay, I'll go catch him before he leaves the scene. He seemed a bit jittery when we rolled up."

"Good," said Grave. "Charlize, are you okay with this?"

She nodded. "Sounds like a plan. Let's get to it."

She motioned for Smithers-Watson to follow, and they both walked off.

"Out of here," said Smithers-Watson, and they were gone.

Morgan looked at Polk. "How long do you need to do your bit?"

Polk bristled. "Well, it's hardly a *bit*. It's more like an exhaustive crime scene and victim analysis."

"Yes, yes," said Morgan. "So when can we get more information?"

Polk cocked his head. "This afternoon, maybe four or so."

Morgan nodded, then turned to Grave. "So let's meet at the station at, say, four-thirty."

Grave shrugged. "Fine." He turned to Loblolly. "Let's find out where this guy lives and then head on out."

"But change first," said Morgan. "And I know where the guy lives. Met him at a cocktail party once. His house is right next to the Hawthorne Mansion, and if anything, it's even bigger."

Grave knew exactly where it was. He had led a murder investigation at the Hawthorne Mansion some years ago. "Right, then." He turned to Loblolly. "Come on, let's get out of these clothes." He regretted the words the moment they came out of his mouth. "No, what I mean is—"

Loblolly laughed. "I know what you mean. Come on, let's do it. Oh, wait, I didn't mean—"

Morgan barked at them. "Just go!"

9

Detective Amanda Snoot followed Grave and Loblolly out to the parking lot and watched as Grave and his drone, Barry, hailed a hovercab and raced out of the parking lot at high speed, leaving Loblolly just standing there in her tight red dress.

Snoot shouted to her. "Hey, how did it go?"

Loblolly walked back to her. Snoot could tell she was not happy. "Ended almost before it began."

"Oh, sorry."

Loblolly shrugged. "Well, at least it's a start. He did like my dress, though."

"He said that? Grave?"

Loblolly shook her head. "No, but I could tell."

"Undressed you with his eyes, eh?"

"Yeah, pretty much." She looked left and right. "Say, did you see my new drone?"

"Sparky? Yeah, she's over there, hailing you a cab."

Loblolly followed Snoot's eyes. "Oh, great. Look, I've got to get home and change, so . . ."

Snoot nodded. "Of course. But let's meet up after this afternoon's meeting. Maybe get a drink or two."

"That sounds great."

"Okay, off you go. Looks like Sparky has a cab for you."

Loblolly turned to see the waiting hovercab, then turned back to Snoot. "See you at the meeting."

"Right."

Loblolly gave her one final nod, then walked across the parking lot to the waiting cab. She said something to Sparky, then both of them got in the cab, which wasted no time accelerating out of the parking lot.

Snoot sighed. *If only I could be a little more like her*, she thought. Loblolly checked every box for beauty and desirability, while Snoot couldn't imagine checking a single one. Thin as a rail with a head too large for her body, she looked like a walking doorknob, a doorknob with rust-colored short hair cut both long and short, as if she had been sheared this way and that by a mischievous child.

She sighed, then looked around the parking lot for the protestor. It didn't take her long to spot him, a short, thin man loading a large sign into the back of an old hovercar.

Well, he is certainly not burdened by money, she thought. He seemed to be in a hurry, so she ran the twenty yards to reach him before he could climb in and hover away. "Hey, you, stop. Crab Cove Police!"

The man, who had just opened the door to the car, stopped immediately and folded his arms over his chest. "What?"

Snoot pulled up in front of him. She was a bit winded by the exertion, but finally managed to find her voice. "Questions. I'd like to ask you a few questions."

The man rolled his eyes, which Snoot noted looked like the Mediterranean Sea. "I have all the licenses. I've done nothing wrong."

"I don't care about your licenses."

He looked confused. "Then what?"

"As I said, questions."

"Look, I'm in a hurry."

"We can do this here or down at the station. Your choice."

The man unexpectedly laughed. Snoot noted the whiteness of his teeth and how small wrinkles appeared around his eyes when he laughed.

"You sound like a bad detective show," he said.

Snoot smiled. "I'll give you that. But you have to give me answers."

The man sighed. "All right, but please, let's do this fast. I'm protesting at a shopping plaza in less than an hour."

Snoot wasn't quite sure what he had just said. She seemed to be focused on him and his good looks and the effect he was having on her. She was feeling a big heat, a heat she had not felt in years.

"So," the man said. "Are you going to ask your questions, or what?"

If she had had her druthers, she would have turned immediately to "or what." But she had questions that had to be answered. "Right, right. Let's start with your name and what you're doing here in this parking lot."

10

The staff break room at the Château de Crabe Rouge smelled of bitter coffee and trenchant ennui. Detective Charlize Holmes, a simdroid who was a perfect match for a young version of actor Charlize Theron and who fancied herself the equal of Sherlock Holmes, pulled up a red plastic chair to one of the dining tables and sat down. Her partner, Dr. Smithers-Watson, who resembled long-dead actor Peter O'Toole but with the voice of another dead actor, Richard Burton, did likewise. As usual, both were dressed in the nineteenth-century garbs of Sherlock Holmes and Dr. Watson.

Charlize nodded at the victim's secretary, Blanche LaTour. "This will do nicely."

Blanche, whose eyes were still red from crying, dabbed at her eyes with a tissue, and sat down opposite them. She was an older woman, perhaps in her early sixties, with a tight bun of gray hair and very little makeup. If Charlize were to guess—which she was loathe to do—she would have said the woman lived for her job and counted the hours when she was away from work, unable to focus on anything else. Although she was thin, she was far from frail. Charlize could tell from the woman's arms that time at the gym may have been her only other activity outside her job. She could also tell that appearance was well down Blanche's priority list. Her dress, a sleeveless black shift, was stylish in a way, but mostly severe, doing nothing to accentuate her body. Her facial expression seemed to be fixed on a deep frown matched by an unflinching stare from her gray eyes, which locked on you and tried to hold you captive or put you on your heels.

Blanche got right to the point. "Who would you like to talk to first?"

"I think we'll start with you, Ms. LaTour."

Blanche blinked. "What, am I a suspect?"

Charlize smiled. "I'm afraid everyone is until we can sort this out."

"But—"

"But I've chosen you first because as Mr. Fontaine's executive secretary, you are more likely to know all or most of the other suspects and Mr. Fontaine's relationship with each."

"Oh. Well. I guess that makes sense."

"Good, good. But before we get to those names, a few preliminary questions."

"Yes, go on."

"How long have you worked for Mr. Fontaine?"

"Seven years."

"And before that."

"Really? Is that pertinent?"

"Perhaps yes, perhaps no, but I will have an answer."

Blanche sighed. "I worked in a similar role at Château du Nez Bleu."

Dr. Smithers-Watson chuckled. "Nez Bleu? The Blue Nose?"

Blanche gave him a weak smile. "After the owner's grandfather, who had a heavily veined and quite bulbous nose."

"A competitor, then."

Blanche nodded. "Of sorts, I guess, but not really. They're a smaller operation and focus on their award-winning pinot noir, which is actually made of grapes. Other than that, their line is mostly fruity wines: apple, blackberry, and so on."

"And you moved to this job because . . . ?"

"I know it must look like a lateral move, but this winery is a much bigger operation, with a greater market share, and it came with the chance to move up."

"Move up? How?"

"Falcon—I mean, Mr. Fontaine—promised me that I could eventually move up to chief of operations or even CEO when the time was right."

"I see," said Charlize. "And in your seven years here, did that opportunity ever present itself?"

Blanche looked down. "It did not." There seemed to be a certain level of resignation in her voice.

"And you resented that?"

Blanche managed a chuckle. "What, are you trying to make me a suspect? I assure you, I did not kill the man. I loved him—in a professional way, of course. He was a complete master, and I've counted myself lucky just to be in his presence."

Charlize detected a note of insincerity in her voice. "But now that he's dead, where does that leave you?"

Blanche blinked, hard. "I don't know. It will depend on his will, I guess."

"Do you have any hopes in that regard?"

She laughed louder. "Of course not. I wasn't in any way considered family by Mr. Fontaine."

"Okay," said Charlize. She turned to Dr. Smithers-Watson. "Any questions for Ms. LaTour?"

Smithers-Watson seemed surprised to be asked. "Well, actually, I do." He turned to Blanche. "Let's get down to some particulars."

"Particulars?"

"Yes, for starters, when was the last time you saw Mr. Fontaine?"

Blanche was quick with her answer. "Yesterday afternoon, late, just before the evening shift came on. He was called to the vineyard floor to inspect a fermentation tank before it came back on line."

"Can you be more precise about the time?"

Blanche looked at the ceiling. "Hmm, I was collecting my things, so it would have been at or near six-thirty, give or take."

"I see, and who made the call to Mr. Fontaine?"

"I have no idea."

"No idea? But who would make such a call?"

"Oh, I see what you mean. Well, it would normally come from the plant engineer. He's responsible for the cleaning of the tanks, so it would have been him or one of his assistants."

Charlize broke in. "And is it normal for the owner to bother with such details?"

Blanche rolled her eyes. "Mr. Fontaine was a perfectionist and very hands-on. He insisted on approving every detail."

"That must have been grating on the staff," said Charlize.

Blanche chortled. "Grating? Oh, more than that. Everyone hated him, detective. Or perhaps *loathed* is a better word."

Charlize sat back in her chair. "Including you, Ms. LaTour?"

She cocked her head. "As I've said, I admired him professionally, but personally, he could be very brutish and callous. So yes, even me, but I didn't kill him."

"Do you know who would?" said Smithers-Watson.

"It's a long list."

Charlize smiled at her. "Shall we begin, then?"

11

Grave was happy to be out of his uncontrollable trousers and into something more familiar: his workaday gray suit. He grabbed a blue tie and began knotting it as he descended from the bedroom to the kitchen.

Roderick was alone now, Horace and Red off to do their own business, so the kitchen was illuminated darkly by Roderick's favorite Surround Vision movie, *Casablanca*. His lookalike, Peter Lorre, was pleading with Humphrey Bogart about something. Grave didn't know what. He had never successfully sat through the movie, not because of its lack of merit, but simply because it was shown in black and white, which gave Grave the creeps. It seemed like a movie best shown in the graveyard.

The thought of the graveyard gave him an idea. After this afternoon's meeting or maybe tomorrow morning, he'd go to the Crab Cove Cinema Cemetery to visit with his ghost friend, Victoria. Perhaps she could shed some light on the murder.

He slipped the tie's knot tight to his throat and continued his descent, finally coming to the ground floor. Red was sitting in a corner, looking forlorn.

"What's up with you?" said Grave.

Red raised his claws and then lowered them. "I've lost my funding."

Grave was stunned. Red was working on an estimated population count of male and female crabs (Jimmies and Sooks) in the Chesapeake Bay. Their numbers were beginning to decline because of climate change, and the estimated count was critical in determining next steps.

"That makes no sense," said Grave.

"Oh, tell me about it."

"But don't they realize how important this is?"

Red scoffed. "Important? Ha! Do you know what they told me?"

"What?"

"Crabs are no longer a priority. Not a priority is what they said. Can you believe that?"

Grave sighed. "And the funding is gone for good?"

Red nodded, which is a difficult thing to do for a simcrab. "For all eternity."

Grave checked his watch. He really needed to get going. He had to pick up Loblolly and head on over to the Fontaine Mansion. "Let me ask you something, Red."

"Of course."

"How much funding were you actually getting, and how much do you really need?"

Red didn't need time to think about it. "About two thousand credits or $20,000 hard cash a year. And that's bare minimum. No frills at all."

"So about two thousand a month?"

"No, more like seventeen hundred."

"Okay, okay, tell you what. Let me see what I can do. If the feds won't come through, perhaps the city council will. Crab Cove is all about crabs, after all."

Red frowned, but Grave probably missed it. A frown is a subtle nuance for a crab, which tends not to express much of anything. "Is it? I wonder. More and more it seems to be that damned Mars Terminal."

He had a point. If foot traffic alone was to be believed, the Mars Terminal was far and away Crab Cove's major attraction now, and the greatest source of its tourist income.

Grave checked his watch again. "Look, I've got to go. Let's talk about this more when I get back. In the meantime, have Roderick transfer four hundred credits from my account to keep you going this week."

Crabs can't smile very well, either, so Red just swung his claws in the air to indicate his pleasure. "Yes!"

Grave laughed. "Okay, get back to work. Now, where is that drone of mine?" He looked around the room and finally spotted Barry hovering near the front door. "There you are. Come on, let's get to it."

"Right," said Barry. "I've called a hovercab."

"Oh, no," said Grave. "No cab this time. We're taking the Sprite."

Barry had learned long ago not to object to the Sprite. He would just have to tune out the gospel music played from the Sprite's radio, at full volume, enough to shake the leaves on the trees and knock unsuspecting birds and insects out of the air.

"As you wish."

Grave started out the door, then stopped and turned back. "Red, have you seen Horace this morning?"

"Yes, he's up on the observation deck, eating a bucket of fries."

"Good," said Grave.

"Do you need him for something?"

"No, just making sure the military hasn't recaptured him."

"He's fine, sir."

Grave turned back to Barry. "Let's go, Barry. Horace is in his French fries and all is right with the world."

"If only," said Barry.

"Come," said Grave. "The Sprite awaits."

It did.

12

Charlize waited until Blanche LaTour had left the break room before speaking.

"Wow, this is quite a list."

"No one liked the man, it seems," said Smithers-Watson. "And we'll never get through that list before this afternoon's meeting."

"Actually, we don't have to. Some of these people are on the evening shift, so we can focus on the staff currently at work, then come back after the meeting, if necessary."

"Sounds good. Where shall we start?"

Charlize looked at the list. "Hmm, how about the assistant vintner, Art Travis Tee."

Smithers-Watson chuckled. "That can't be his real name."

"Oh, I'm sure it is. There seems to be no end to how humans abuse their children."

"It's a double whammy, really."

"What do you mean?"

"Well, first you have his full name, which is ridiculous. Obviously, the poor boy would not want to ever introduce himself that way."

"I see what you mean. He could go with an initial for his middle name."

"But that makes him Art T. Tee, as in Arty Tee or Art tee-tee. Not exactly powerful names."

"And if he drops the middle initial, he's just Art Tee, or Arty."

"Wait, how many whammies does that make?"

"Four, I think."

"Wait, there's at least one more. He could just call himself Mr. Tee, as in 'I pity the fool' Mr. T."

Charlize shook her head. "His parents should be shot."

"I wonder what their names are. Maybe they were screwed by their parents as well, and are just passing the problem along to the next generation."

"I don't want to think about it. Now, let's get Art in here."

"Right." Smithers-Watson pressed the button on the intercom. "Will Mr. Tee please come to the break room?" He could hear his own voice echo throughout the facility, followed by a sound that was unmistakable: laughter.

A minute later, the door swung open and a man looking none too pleased walked in and sat down without a word opposite them.

Charlize looked down at the list. "You are Art Travis Tee?"

The man nodded and then folded his arms across his chest.

"Well, Mr. Tee, we'd—"

"Stop right there. Call me Bubba."

Charlize looked over at Smithers-Watson, who from his expression—a smile threatening to explode into a guffaw—had no doubt framed a response suitable for Bubba Tee. She tried her best not to chuckle, and pressed on, trying to take in this man of cursed names.

Bubba was not what she expected. She expected to see a small man, perhaps with wireless-rim glasses. He'd be bald and fastidious, always in a white lab coat and always focused on the job.

Instead, the man before her was a giant of a man. Take off his lumberjack-red plaid shirt and you'd see Conan the Barbarian. His hair was thick and black and combed strait back, a perfect counterpoint to his black bushy beard. Within that frame of black was an axe-like nose and eyes as close to turquoise as she'd ever seen.

"Okay, um, Bubba, when was the last time you saw Mr. Fontaine?"

Bubba rolled his eyes. "So I'm a suspect, am I?" His voice was deep and threatening.

Charlize cocked her head. "We're interviewing everyone, Bubba. Trying to piece together where everyone was at the time of the crime."

"So I *am* a suspect."

"If you want to think of it that way, fine, but I assure you, we're just collecting information at this point."

Bubba unfolded his arms, and seemed to relax. "All right, let me just say straight off what anyone here will tell you. I hated the man. The things he was doing to the wine were unconscionable. And as to your question, the last time I saw the bastard was yesterday morning, at our normal time for checking the status of the new batch of wine."

"And what time would that have been?"

"Just after 6:30 a.m."

"And how did that go?"

"Quietly. We've pretty much stopped speaking to one another."

"You mentioned being at odds over the wine."

"He relied too much on nanobots."

"Nanobots? How was he using them?"

"In the worst possible way. Anyone who tastes our wine, regardless of the natural tendencies of their taste buds, will love our wine."

Smithers-Watson leaned forward. "You mean the nanobots *force* people to like the wine?"

Bubba nodded. "In a manner of speaking."

"Surely that can't be legal," said Charlize.

Bubba laughed sardonically. "It's a gray area. Nanobots were introduced with great fanfare a decade ago, when we still made wine out of grapes. Their function then was to neutralize sulfites and—not to be too technical—to *smooth* the wine."

"And what was your alternative to nanobots?"

"Oh, I'd still use nanobots, but not the taste czars he was using."

"How so?"

"My nanobots would smooth the wine—their original function—without making *everyone* love the wine. I mean, how can you take pride in a product you know everyone *must* like?"

Charlize nodded. "I see. And this last meeting, how did that go?"

Bubba shrugged. "Routine. Less than a minute, really. Everything was going according to plan—*his* plan."

Smithers-Watson interrupted. "And there was no meeting with him this morning?"

"No."

"And what did you think about that? Did you not think that odd?"

Bubba shook his head. "I looked at it like a blessing, a little vacation from him."

Charlize nodded. "Okay, and what about the rest of the day?"

"Today, you mean?"

"Yes."

Bubba shrugged. "Been here, doing my job."

Charlize looked at Smithers-Watson. "Anything else?"

He shook his head.

"Okay," said Charlize. "Thank you for your time, Bubba. I only ask that you not discuss our conversation with anyone else here and that you make yourself available for future talks."

"Can I go home after my shift?"

"Yes, of course. We have your contact information. If we need you, we'll be in touch."

Bubba nodded and pushed back his chair. "I hated the man, but I didn't kill him."

Charlize nodded back. "Of course."

Bubba turned, lumbered across the room, and left.

Charlize turned to Smithers-Watson. "What do you think?"

"Bibbitee, bobbitee, bubbatee."

13

Any normal antique Austin Healey Sprite that had been converted to electric power would have glided down the highway with barely a whisper. But not Grave's. His car had a flaw: its radio was stuck at full volume on a gospel station that featured the one-minute sermons of the late Reverend Bendigo Bottoms, now a feature attraction at the Crab Cove Cinema Cemetery, where the deceased lived on, even thrived, through videos recorded before their deaths.

Grave glanced over at Polly Loblolly. She was dressed in her business clothes now, a gray pants suit that struggled to camouflage the beautiful woman within. He thought to compliment her, but knew she wouldn't be able to hear him. The gospel music played on, Polly completely unaware under the noise-cancelling headphones Grave had provided.

He turned his attention back to the road. He could see the Hawthorne Mansion ahead and knew that the Fontaine Mansion lay just beyond it. The two structures couldn't have been any more different, the Hawthorne Mansion a textbook brick structure in the Georgian style and the Fontaine Mansion an homage to glass and triangles. I. M. Pei would have found it too modern for his tastes.

Grave slowed the Sprite and coasted down the winding driveway into a cantilevered glass portico. He turned off the car and tapped Polly on the shoulder. "We're here."

Polly looked confused, then realized Grave was talking to her. She took off the headphones. "So, this is it?"

"Yes, in all its splendor."

Polly looked around. "Splendor is not the word for it. It looks like someone glued together shards of broken glass."

Grave chuckled. "It does." He opened his car door and began the process of extricating his long limbs from the tiny Sprite.

Polly did the same. "Wow, getting out is easier said than done."

"You'll get used to it."

"Oh, I doubt that."

Grave waited for her to get out, then pointed at the stairs to the door. "Let's go. I'll break the news to them, but they may need a woman's touch after that."

Polly rolled her eyes. "Grave, I've done this many times. I know what to expect."

"Right, right. Anyway, I'll do it this time."

They walked up the steps, and Grave pushed the doorbell button. The sound of trumpets followed, a blast of sound that nearly knocked them back down the stairs.

"Well, our presence is known, that's for sure."

Polly laughed. "Why would they need that so loud?"

"Maybe they're hard of hearing. Then again, this place is so big they might need trumpets to know anyone was at their door."

Polly pointed at the glass door. "Here we go."

Grave could see a woman walking toward them. The way she walked seemed familiar. Very familiar. "No, it can't be."

"What?"

"Her, the woman. She reminds me of someone I used to know."

"Probably just your imagination."

The woman grew closer to the door, her features growing clearer with each step.

"Oh, my god," said Grave.

"Grave, what's wrong. You look like you've seen a ghost."

Grave was hyperventilating. "This can't be happening."

Polly didn't know what to say, but she did know Grave was in no shape to notify the family of Fontaine's death. "Step behind me," she said. "I'll handle this."

Grave did as she said, hiding behind Polly and looking over her shoulder as the door swung open. The woman spotted him instantly. "Oh, my god. Simon? Is that you?"

Grave stepped from behind Polly. "Yes, Lola."

"Good to see you," she said. "I guess you're here to tell me about the death of my dear father."

Grave blinked. "Your father?"

"Yes."

Grave stood there looking at her.

"So," she said, "are you going to introduce me to your colleague?"

Grave stammered. "Um, um . . ."

She rolled her eyes. "Oh, good grief." She extended her hand to Polly. "Hi, I'm Lola LaFarge. Simon and I used to be lovers."

Now it was time for Polly to blink, hard.

14

Angus McBride, the winery's maintenance engineer, walked into the breakroom with a frown on his face and a swagger in his walk that suggested a mixture of defiance, impatience, and menace.

He was a short man and stocky, with oversized forearms earned by twisting valves on and off. His face was broad and pocked with the scars of his teenage years. Large black brows waggled and arched as he took in Charlize and Smithers-Watson for the first time, his pale blue eyes dancing from one to the other.

He stopped in front of the table and pulled out the chair. "So, this about Fontaine?" The words came out like a snarl.

"Indeed," said Charlize. "Have a seat."

He sat down and looked from one to the other. "Simdroids, right?"

"Yes," said Smithers-Watson. "Do you have a problem with that?"

McBride shook his head. "Of course not. I have several simdroids working for me. None dressed as strangely as you guys, though."

Charlize ignored the comment. "Well, then, shall we get started?"

McBride shrugged. "Whatever, but you're wasting your time talking to me. I hated the man—we all did—but I didn't kill him."

"Of course you didn't," said Charlize. "But we're talking to everyone, trying to get both a sense of the man and who might have had a reason to kill him."

"We all have our reasons."

"And yours would be . . ." said Smithers-Watson.

"Two gripes, really. First, he never budgeted enough money to maintain the equipment properly, to replace it when necessary, and so on."

"And second?" said Charlize.

McBride slumped back in his chair. "I haven't had a raise for eight years. Do you know what that means in this economy?"

Charlize nodded. "Difficult times."

McBride scoffed. "You think? I can't afford anything. I'm strung out, and I'm not the only one. He was a right skinflint."

"I see," said Smithers-Watson, "but why not move on, get a job with a competitor?"

McBride rolled his eyes. "Don't you think I've tried? No, the only competitor out there is Château du Nez Bleu, and they're an all-simdroid operation."

"I see," said Charlize. "Perhaps the new owner will be more open to increasing your wages. Whoever it is will want to retain staff, I would think."

McBride seemed to brighten. "That's what me and the others think, too. I tell you, it could be a blessing, Fontaine's death."

Charlize and Smithers-Watson stared back at him.

"I mean when we look on the bright side. Like I said, I didn't kill him."

"Yes, you've said that," said Charlize. "Now, one last question, at least for now."

"Go on."

"When was the last time you saw Mr. Fontaine?"

"Yesterday evening. He stormed past me on the way to inspect a fermentation tank. He seemed very angry, so I gave him wide berth."

"Angry," said Smithers-Watson. "Do you know what about?"

McBride shook his head. "No, but it could have been anything. Anger was his go-to emotion. At least in my experience."

"All right," said Charlize. "We may have additional questions in the coming days. Please make yourself available, and don't leave Crab Cove."

McBride shook his head. "Me? Leave? I can't *afford* to leave this damned town." He pushed back in his chair, stood, and left the room.

"What do you think?" said Smithers-Watson.

"No raise for eight years? I'd think that situation would have come to a head long ago. No, on the face of it, I don't think he's our man. Still, until we know more about Fontaine's death, we'll keep him on the list."

15

Grave and Loblolly were both having trouble dealing with the woman standing before them. Grave didn't know how to handle seeing his ex again, and Loblolly was struggling with images of Grave and this Lola person making love.

Loblolly could see how this stunningly beautiful woman would check every box for Grave. Eyes, large and brown, somewhere between walnut and hazelnut. Eyebrows, thin and shaped and plucked to near nonexistence. Nose, small and turned up. Skin, pale as parchment. Lips, full and pouty. Hair, chestnut brown and short. Body, petite and toned. Breasts, abundant. Smile, disarming. Neck, long and almost regal. Waist, thin. Hips, ample. Ass, a marvel. And legs, perfect. All this gift-wrapped in a tight green sweater and black yoga pants that left little to the imagination.

Lola smiled at her, knowing she was being sized up. "I'm sorry you had to come all this way. Dad's executive secretary, Blanche, gave me a heads up about an hour ago."

Loblolly looked at Grave, who was still staring into space, not sure what to do or say.

"So," Loblolly said, "you seem to be handling it well."

Lola shrugged. "We weren't close."

"But you're here, at his house."

Lola looked around. "Not for long. Too much glass for my tastes."

Loblolly smiled. "It is a bit much, isn't it?"

Lola ignored the question. She looked at Grave and then back at Loblolly. "He'll come out of it in a minute. You may not know this, but he hates surprises and he's not good at emotions."

Loblolly couldn't help chuckling. "Yeah, I've kind of noticed that."

"So how long have you guys been together?"

Loblolly could feel herself blush. "Um, we're just colleagues."

Lola rolled her eyes. "Okay, I'll play along." She looked back at Grave. "Looks like he's finally coming out of it."

Grave took a deep breath and let it out slowly.

"There he is," said Lola. "Right on schedule." She snapped her fingers in front of his face. "Grave, *Grave*, we're over here."

Grave brushed her hand away. "I can see that. Now, is there some place we can talk?"

"Of course," said Lola. "My brother is in the library, so we might as well go there. I'm sure you'll want to talk to him as well." She stepped back and motioned them down a long glass hallway.

Grave and Loblolly followed her, Grave's attention focused on Lola and the movement of her hips. As they walked, Loblolly gave him sidelong glances, trying to assess his reaction to seeing Lola gain.

He seemed transfixed.

Loblolly assessed the situation with a single thought. *Shit!*

16

Detective Amanda Snoot assessed the situation with a single thought. *Wow!*

She was completely enamored of this man in the parking lot. The more she talked to him, the more she wanted to talk to him. His name was Harry Smite and he was president of a one-person nonprofit dedicated to restoring the grape to its traditional place in winemaking. His distaste for grapeless wine and their makers was palpable.

"This Fontaine person was evil, reprehensible, a scourge on our planet. I cheer his death, celebrate it. It's a victory for grapes everywhere."

Snoot didn't like the idea that this man was now a prime suspect for the murder, so she tried her best to extricate him from suspicion.

"But you wouldn't kill him, would you?" she said, nodding her head, hoping he'd follow the gesture with an *of course not.*

But he didn't. "He deserved it. Drowned in his own foul solution. I can't think of a more appropriate death."

"Actually, he was stabbed—several times."

Smite laughed and pulled a Bowie knife out of a sheath strapped to his right leg. "You mean with a knife like this?"

Snoot took a step back. "Whoa, put that away."

He didn't. Instead, he made stabbing motions in the air. "Now *this* is a knife!"

Snoot held up her hands and backed away. "Whoa, whoa, stop that."

"Slice, stab, slice," he screamed, waving the knife around.

Snoot rolled her eyes, then stepped forward, grabbed his knife arm, and flipped him to the ground with a long-practiced karate move.

He hit the ground hard, the knife falling from his grasp and skittering a few feet away. "Hey, what are you doing?"

"Harry Smite, I should damn well arrest you for wielding a knife of illegal length in public and for suspicion of murder . . . ."

Smite's eyes went wide. "But you're not going to, right? I was just clowning around."

"I should, I really should." Instead, she gave him her hand and pulled him to his feet. "But consider this a warning, and lose that knife. If I see it ever again, you'll be behind bars."

17

The library was the strangest Grave and Loblolly had ever seen. Instead of the usual reading pods, where readers could create their own reading environment—imagery and sounds to best match the topic—there were glass shelves containing hundreds of last-edition books actually made of paper. Grave and Loblolly had both seen single examples of this old technology, but never so many volumes in one place.

Lola noticed their rapt attention to the books. "My father's silly hobby. He thought they'd grow in value, so he spent a good part of his vast fortune tracking down and acquiring these oddities."

Grave moved closer to the shelves and noticed that they were actually cases—the books were sealed within. "And he couldn't actually read them."

Lola chuckled. "He could have, but they would have crumbled to dust." She shrugged. "Now they're just entombed, protected by a blend of inert gases. Barring leaks, they should last a few more centuries."

"It's sad, really," said Loblolly. "I remember my mother trying to read one to me. It just didn't compare to the pod experience, so I ran away every time she tried to read to me. It seemed like a punishment somehow."

Lola smiled at her. "I had much the same experience, except my mother actually caught me. It's funny, I can't remember her face, but I do remember how tight she held me."

Grave suddenly startled. He'd just noticed a man sitting in the room with them. "You must be the brother."

The man, who was sitting in a high-backed leather wingchair, uncrossed his legs and then re-crossed them. Grave could see the resemblance to the father, but the man before him was thinner, almost skeletal. From the crow's feet around the man's eyes, he could tell he was the older brother of Lola. His hair was the same color as Lola's but cut short, the hair a mere shadow on his head. Unlike Lola, he had blue eyes. A nose like a knife cut his face in half, a hollow cheek on either side. Frowning seemed to be his go-to expression.

"And the son," the man said. His voice was high-pitched, almost feminine. "Frankie Fontaine. I suppose you're here about dad."

"Yes," said Grave. "We came to break the news about his murder, but I guess the news got here before we did."

Frankie snorted. "Good news travels fast."

Loblolly cocked her head. "I take it there was no love lost between you and your father."

"Oh, no, no, no. To be lost, love must first be given. And that was never the case."

Loblolly raised an eyebrow. "That seems a bit harsh."

"You didn't know my father." He turned to Lola. "Tell him, Lola."

Lola sighed. "He was a right bastard, that man. To both of us. Not that he was singling us out. He was a bastard to everyone, and I'm happy he's dead." She paused. "No, I'm *thrilled* that he's dead. The world is in a better place now."

Grave nodded. "Perhaps we can get into that as we pursue the murderer."

Lola snorted. "Well, you certainly have a long list of likely suspects."

"Including you," said Loblolly. "And your brother here."

Frankie laughed. "Oh, my dear woman. If I had any intention of killing him, I would have done it when I was twelve. Yes, he was awful to us, always, but that was the norm for me and Lola. His wrath was just an unpleasant background to our lives."

"Even so," said Grave. "We'll need a full accounting of your whereabouts over the past twenty-four hours."

Lola rolled her eyes. "You can't be serious."

"I can," said Grave. "And if you're innocent, you shouldn't mind."

Lola huffed. "But you know me, Simon. You know I'm not capable of murder."

Grave nodded. "I would hope that is the case, Lola, but we'll be asking the questions anyway."

Lola shook her head, clearly disgusted. "Well, then, let's get on with it." She crossed the room to sit in the wingchair next to Frankie's. "Come, have a seat. We have nothing to hide."

Grave and Loblolly sat down on a loveseat opposite them.

"All right," said Grave. "Who wants to go first?"

18

Charlize and Smithers-Watson were about to wrap up the initial interviews when a tall man in a pale blue jumpsuit walked into the breakroom.

"Here now," he said. "I hope you're not leaving. Be a shame to miss a prime suspect like me."

Charlize smiled back at him. "And you would be?"

"Nigel Forthwith the Third."

"That sounds very British, but you don't sound British."

Forthwith shrugged. "I can fake it a bit, if you like, but it comes out all wrong."

"Not necessary," said Smithers-Watson. "And why would you be a prime suspect?"

"Yes," said Charlize. "Why?"

"Wow, I thought I'd be at the top of the list. I'm the labor organizer here and a major thorn in the rump of Mr. Fontaine. Or at least I was."

"But let me guess," said Charlize. "You didn't kill him."

"Exactly, said Forthwith. "But I'd like to at least be considered a suspect. My workers would expect that of me."

"So, you didn't kill him, but you wish you had?"

Forthwith shrugged. "No, no, I wouldn't wish death on anyone, even that bastard Fontaine. It's just that I have an image to uphold."

"I see," said Charlize. "All right, have a seat. We'll run you through the questions and see what's what."

"Excellent," said Forthwith, taking the chair opposite them. "So, who have you interviewed so far?"

Charlize looked down at her notes. "Let's see. Bubba Tee for one."

"Bubba Bobitty Boo? Definitely a prime suspect."

"Yes, maybe, and Angus McBride, the maintenance engineer."

Forthwith screwed up his face. "Nah, doesn't have the balls."

"Thanks for the analysis," said Smithers-Watson.

"You're welcome," said Forthwith. "Who else?"

"A few of the simdroids," said Charlize.

"Nah again," said Forthwith. "Balls have been programmed out of them. Very compliant, them. Don't hate or hold grudges. Nose to the grindstone, them."

"So we thought, too," said Charlize.

"Well, then, you said you had questions. Come on, have at me. I promise you I won't disappoint."

"Very well," said Charlize. "Please reconstruct your past twenty-four hours for us. Where were you and what were you doing? Be as specific as you can. Who you were with and so on."

"That's a big first question."

"They're all big questions. So . . ."

Forthwith took a deep breath. "Well, then, here goes. Twenty-four hours ago I was sitting in this very room, haggling with Fontaine over the terms of a new labor agreement."

"Was it a cordial meeting?" said Charlize.

Forthwith's laugh was almost a bark. "Cordial? Oh, hell no."

19

Lola LaFarge tried to be cordial, but Grave could tell she was struggling to keep control. There was something odd about her posture, for one. She was sitting across from him with her legs locked tight together and her hands clasped together and held firmly against her thighs. Her back was straight, and she was holding her head high, chin up. The overall look reminded Grave of a Viking-horned opera singer about to break into some sad, somber song. His single thought: *she's hiding something.*

"So, if I'm hearing you correctly, you were both here, in the mansion, all day yesterday."

Lola and her brother Frankie looked at one another and then nodded. "Yes," they said, almost in unison.

But then Lola added, "Mostly."

"Mostly?"

Lola turned to Frankie. "You remember, right, we took a drive?"

Frankie looked confused, but then said, "Oh, right, the drive."

"Where to," said Grave, "and when?"

"Just around—to get the hell out of this glass house, really."

"Yes," said Frankie. "A little drive is all, in the afternoon."

"Can you give me a time?"

"Six-ish, maybe," said Lola.

"But no destination?"

"No," said Frankie.

Grave looked back and forth between them. Their story seemed odd, and they were blinking too much to be telling the truth.

"No destination at all?" said Loblolly, who had been oddly quiet during most of the conversation. She seemed to be spending most of her time staring at Grave staring at Lola, and she was clearly not happy.

Lola shrugged. "No, just a break from all this glass. As I've told you, I returned from France at the request of my father, who wanted me to sort through my things so he could repurpose my room. That has taken all my time, and once that's done, I'll be going back to France."

"You'll be staying for the funeral, though," said Loblolly.

Lola blinked as if she hadn't considered that possibility. "Um, yes, of course." She looked extremely nervous. "When do you think that might be?"

"I'm not sure," said Grave. "We'll be meeting with the medical examiner after we finish up here. Until he's finished with his work, the body will remain at the morgue."

"Could you at least hazard a guess?" said Frankie. "We need to make arrangements."

"Understood," said Grave. "In most cases, the body is released a day or so after the formal autopsy and receipt of the toxicology reports."

Frankie frowned. "So we're talking about, what, a week?"

"Or ten days," said Grave. "That or thereabouts."

Frankie slumped back in his seat and heaved a weighty sigh. "That long, eh?"

Grave nodded.

"Another question for you," said Loblolly. "This is a very big house. How many servants do you have?"

Lola was at a loss. "I'm not sure. Frankie?"

"There's seven full-time to take care of us and the house, as well as a part-time gardener. Dad wasn't into vegetation."

"I see," said Loblolly.

Grave looked at his watch. "We may want to speak with them at some point."

Lola started wringing her hands. "Is that necessary?"

"Perhaps not. We'll let you know. For now, we'll let you get back to sorting out that room of yours."

"We're done then?" said Lola.

"Yes," said Grave. "For now."

Lola tried very hard to suppress a smile, but Grave saw it, and so did Loblolly.

"Well, then," said Lola, standing. "I'll show you out."

She escorted them through the maze of glass walls and out the front door.

Grave turned to thank her, but she had already turned on her heels and walked away.

He looked at Loblolly. "Well, that was rather abrupt."

"Yes," said Loblolly. "But not unexpected. She was very defensive in there."

"She was," said Grave. "I've never seen her so nervous."

"Hiding something perhaps."

"Yes, but what? I can't believe she would be capable of murder."

"I don't think you're being objective, Simon."

Grave sighed. "Maybe not."

"And there's one other thing I'd like you to explain to me."

"Oh, and what is that?"

"Why on earth did you affect a British accent while we were in there?"

"What? Really?"

"Yes."

Grave sighed. He thought he and his therapist had solved that problem years ago. "There was a time, believe it or not, when I thought, at least subconsciously, that a British accent made me appear more intelligent. I haven't lapsed into that for years. Not since . . ."

"Not since you were with Lola, right?"

Grave blinked. She was right. "Yes, not since then."

Loblolly shrugged. "I wouldn't worry about it. Probably just the shock of seeing her again."

Grave considered it. "Yes, maybe."

"So, do you still have feelings for her?"

Grave didn't know how to answer, but realized he'd have to say something. "Well . . ."

Loblolly rolled her eyes and started walking away. "Not important. Let's get to that meeting."

Grave watched her walk away, then slowly followed. His one thought: *Shite!*

20

Loblolly was happy to be back in the Sprite and under her headphones. Grave couldn't talk to her even if he wanted to, and that was just fine with her. As they drove, she tried her best to keep her eyes on the road, but she could not resist occasional sidelong glances at Grave. Maddeningly, he seemed to be happy. Or maybe it was just whatever gospel song was playing. She could see the leaves shaking on the trees as they sped by, an indication that the song was as emotionally charged as it was deafening.

She'd have to talk to him as soon as the car and the radio stopped. He clearly still had feelings for Lola LaFarge, and Loblolly didn't want to be a witness to that. She needed space, time to think things through while he sorted out whatever was going on inside his head. She'd request to be re-united with her partner, Detective Snoot. He could pull Sergeant Blunt back in as his partner or opt to team up with that strange Officer Larry, in whatever incarnation of being he was now acting out, whether it was God or some other role played by Morgan Freeman, his lookalike.

As the car sped on, her decision became firm. She couldn't do this anymore. Not while he was being indecisive. Let someone else control his British accent. Lola had set it off, obviously, so maybe she knew how to bring him back to his own voice.

Loblolly glanced over at Grave, who was smiling and staring at her. *What a dolt*, she thought. *Does he have no idea how much he hurt me with his fawning display with Lola?*

She frowned at him and turned back to stare at the road. *Let him think about that look*, she thought. She waited a few seconds and then glanced back at him. He had a look of extreme puzzlement on his face. *What an idiot!*

She growled in frustration but couldn't hear the growl. There was just a vibration in her throat that she hoped Grave could sense as well. He would have at least seen her face contort. *Good.*

Finally, the police station came into view. She tried to compose herself for the speech she had in mind. She would be cool and calm. Professional as hell. And if he refused her request, she would go to Captain Morgan.

The car came to a stop in Grave's reserved spot, and she began extricating her long limbs from the car. A less athletic woman would have tumbled out of the car onto the pavement, but Loblolly managed to get out in one fluid movement.

Grave, long practiced in the art of Sprite extrication, was already out of the car, patiently waiting for her, and she was ready for him. The first few words of the planned speech came to mind: *Sir, I respectfully ask to be reassigned back to my partner, Detective Snoot.*

Instead, what came out was, "You son of a bitch!"

And then she turned on her heels and ran for the station door.

"Loblolly, wait," he said, but he knew his words came out too late and far too British.

21

Captain Morgan rocked back and forth in his large leather office chair, one of his perks of office, and listened patiently to Officer Larry. The simdroid, who like all the other simdroid Officer Larrys, looked just like the late actor Morgan Freeman, was different in one respect: he was the first Officer Larry promoted to the rank of detective. As such, he needed to switch out of his uniform into something more appropriate for a detective. He also was charged by Captain Morgan to come up with a new name and identity, so he would stand out from all the other Officer Larrys.

And that's where the problems had begun. His first thought was to identify with the roles played by Freeman in his many movies. He was God for a time, and then Dr. Alex Cross. Neither choice seemed right, so he tried being Mark Twain for a while. And although he peppered his conversations with Twain quotes where appropriate, the persona just didn't catch on, particularly with Captain Morgan.

Morgan stopped rocking and leaned across the desk toward Officer Larry, who was now dressed minimally as Gandhi. "This won't do."

"But he's famous."

Morgan screwed up his face. "I can't have you wandering around Crab Cove almost naked."

"But—"

"No, the answer is no. Now, let's make this simple, shall we?"

"Simple?"

"No famous people. You're famous enough looking like Morgan Freeman. How about just being Morgan Freeman, the off-camera one, not the actor."

Larry looked troubled. "I have no idea how to do that."

"Turn around," said Morgan, pointing through the glass wall of his office toward the squad room. Several uniformed Officer Larrys were scurrying around the room, doing their work.

"What?"

"Look at your fellow officers. Are they being actor Morgan Freeman?"

"Um, no."

"Exactly. They're being Morgan Freeman being a police officer. Now, you need to do that."

"But you said not to wear my uniform."

Morgan puffed out a breath. Larry wasn't getting it. "No, what I mean is just wear slacks and a sport coat and be Detective Larry. You don't have to be God. You don't have to be Mark Twain. Just be you."

"Me? I'm not sure what that means."

Morgan rolled his eyes. "Just be the guy who helped us solve those murders in Town Square."

"The invisible bodies?"

"Yeah, that guy. You were great at being that guy."

"But my programming has been supplemented to include every role played by Freeman. Is it okay if I at least quote from those roles from time to time?"

Morgan threw up his hands. "Of course, of course."

"And can I wear clothes like Alex Cross? I really liked wearing those vests."

"Yes, yes, that's the ticket. Now, you go and change. We have a meeting in just a few minutes about this winery murder, and I want you to be part of that investigation."

"I have the clothes in my locker, so I'll change immediately. But one last thing."

"Yes?"

I don't want to be Detective Larry. I want to be Detective Morgan Freeman. If I'm going to be the man, I want his name as well."

Morgan rubbed a hand over his bald head, considering the request. "We'll give it a trial period. If there's no confusion about Morgan you and Morgan me, we'll lock it in."

Newly named Detective Freeman beamed. "Yes, sir." He stood and reached across the desk to shake Morgan's hand.

Captain Morgan gave it a good shake. "Now go change. I don't want you to miss a single minute of this meeting."

"Yes, sir. Yes, sir." He backed out of the office, then turned and ran for the locker room.

Morgan began rocking again, but not for long. He could see an angry Detective Loblolly striding toward his office. His single thought: *Shit!*

22

Captain Morgan and Detective Loblolly were the last to enter the conference room. Loblolly avoided eye contact with everyone and slipped into a chair near the head of the long table. Morgan stood with his hands on the back of his chair at the head of the table, looking from one detective to the next, making sure everyone was present. When he came to Detective Morgan Freeman, he gave him a nod and a smile—the clothing Freeman had selected could best be called Alex Cross Casual: a pale blue shirt unbuttoned at the top along with a blue and gray sweater vest with a herringbone pattern.

Morgan cleared his throat. "All here, good. As you can probably guess, because of Mr. Fontaine's status in the community—meaning he was rich as hell—the mayor has taken a special interest in this case." He put "special interest" in air quotes, which prompted laughter around the table.

"What that means is that we do our jobs the way we do our jobs: thoroughly and efficiently and with no bowing down to pressure. We'll get this guy—*our* way."

Medical Examiner Jeremy Polk raised a hand, and Morgan acknowledged him. "Yes, Polk?"

"Can we get on with it? I've got another body to deal with."

Grave, who had been studying Loblolly's face, trying to read her, without success, perked up. "Another body?"

"Yes," said Polk. "A Mrs. Hannah Wiggle, murdered in her home just last evening."

Grave turned to Morgan. "Shall we split up the teams to work on this new case?"

Morgan shook his head. "No, already handled."

"Handled? How? Who?"

"Sergeant Blunt has taken over the investigation, with the help of some young private investigators."

"Private investigators?"

"Yes, from a new outfit, Red Owl Investigations, owned and operated by Penelope Goodlove and assisted by Sergeant Blunt's daughter, Rippley Blunt."

Grave blinked. "But they're just children."

Morgan frowned. "Look, we can discuss this further after this meeting. The point is I will not divert any of you to help with that case, at least not now. Understood?" He looked around the room, satisfied by the nods he was receiving. He turned to Polk. "All right, Jeremy, you're on."

Polk stood up, making him just a tad taller than he was while sitting down, and walked to the front of the room. "First and foremost, let me put to rest the question that is probably in everyone's mind here. Serial killer Chester Clink was not involved with this murder. The knife wounds are inconsistent with his preferred knife and method of attack."

"But they *are* knife wounds, right?" said Charlize.

"Yes, absolutely, but nothing like the damage inflicted by Clink's Bowie knife. The knife here was small and thin-bladed."

"How small?" asked Smithers-Watson.

"Given the depths of the wounds, I'd say smaller than a steak knife."

"You mean like an every-day-carry knife?"

Polk nodded. "An EDC knife would fit the bill, yes, although I would not rule out other short-bladed knives. A paring knife, for example."

Detective Morgan Freeman spoke up. "Small knives like that seem odd choices for a murder."

"Indeed," said Polk, "but the murderer wielded it with a frenzy. There are thirty-two wounds on the body. Six of them are defensive wounds on the hands and forearms. Twenty-five of them are thrusts to the chest. And the final one, the death blow, a slash across the throat that severed the jugular with surgical precision."

Loblolly raised her hand, but avoided looking at anyone sitting at the table. She kept her eyes focused on Polk. "So drowning is out of the question as cause of death?"

"Oh, yes," said Polk. "There was no blood outside the tank, so my assumption is that he was killed in the tank while it was empty. And then the killer flooded the tank, leading to the dispersion of blood."

"What about time of death?" said Morgan. "Can you give us a window?"

Polk smiled. "It was a challenge, but I was able to calculate the rate of blood dispersion in the wine with some precision. Now, assuming the time between Fontaine's death and his deposit in the tank was just a few minutes or so—which seems reasonable—I would place time of death at or near 6:45 p.m. yesterday."

Charlize raised a hand. "According to the maintenance engineer, Fontaine would have been there—along with the maintenance engineer—to inspect the cleaning of the tank."

"And," said Smithers-Watson, "according to the assistant vintner, who saw Fontaine heading that way, Fontaine was angry."

"So," said Morgan, "is it possible we already have our man, meaning the maintenance engineer?"

Charlize shrugged. "His presence at the tank so close to the time of death would suggest that, but based on our preliminary interviews, there's reason to suspect several people."

"Right," said Smithers-Watson. "Everyone seemed to hate the man, and every person we talked to had specific grievances against him."

Grave spoke up. "And we'll have to add his son to that list, too."

Loblolly gave him a fierce look. "And his daughter, Lola LaFarge, as well."

Grave started to object, but Morgan interrupted him. "Grave, you mean *your* Lola LaFarge?"

Grave blushed. "She's not my Lola anymore. Haven't seen her in years—until today." He nodded at Loblolly. "And Loblolly is correct. We'll have to consider her a suspect as well, although I personally would find that hard to believe."

Morgan nodded and then turned to the others at the table. "Any other prime suspects?"

Detective Snoot raised her hand. "Not exactly a prime suspect, but certainly a man we should consider. A protestor who has been lurking around the vineyard for several days. Name's Harry Smite, of Save the Grapes."

"Okay," said Morgan. "Anyone else?"

Smithers-Watson pulled out his fact recorder and stood up. "Blanche LaTour, his executive secretary, and Nigel Forthwith III, the labor leader at the vineyard."

"Okay," said Morgan. "Let's start digging deeper into all of them. Where were they? Do they have alibis?"

"Right," said Grave. "Opportunity is key here, since all of them seem to have motive enough. Loblolly and I will focus on the family, and—"

"No," said Morgan, firmly. "I'd like to reform our traditional teams: Charlize and Smithers-Watson, Snoot and Loblolly, and You and—eventually—Blunt. But since Blunt is busy on another case, I'd like you to team up with our newest detective, who has finally settled on a persona: Detective Morgan Freeman."

Freeman smiled and waved his hand. "Just call me Morgan."

"Or *Freeman*," said Captain Morgan, "so there's no confusion."

Freeman nodded. "Yes, of course."

Grave thought to object, but he could tell by the expression on Morgan's face—and especially Loblolly's—that he should accept the decision.

"All right," he said. "Let's get back out there first thing in the morning. Follow up with everyone and look for other possible suspects as well. We'll meet again this time tomorrow to go over our progress." He turned to Morgan. "Anything else, sir?"

Morgan shook his head, but then changed his mind. "Um, yes. If anyone has a major breakthrough, let me and Grave know. If we can wrap this up sooner rather than later, my stomach—and our damned mayor—will thank you."

Everyone started to leave, but Polk began waving his arms. "Wait, I'm not finished."

Everyone stopped, but no one returned to their seats.

"Seriously," said Polk. "You people have a way of charging out the door half informed."

"All right," said Morgan. "What is it?"

Polk took a deep breath. "Two things. First, the many wounds were made in a frenzy, except for one. The throat was cut slowly, like the murderer was enjoying watching the man die, and didn't want to rush it. So the first wounds brought him down, subdued him enough to finish him off. Anger first and almost a glee after."

"Not surprising," said Charlize. "I can see several of our suspects doing that. As we've all said, the man was hated, truly hated."

Polk nodded. "And one other very interesting thing." He stopped to make sure they were paying attention.

"Come on, Jeremy," said Morgan. "Get on with it."

"The preliminary toxicology report revealed that Fontaine was being slowly poisoned."

"Whoa," said Grave. "What poison are we talking about?"

"Thycrabadol."

"Wait, what?" said Morgan. "What's that?"

"It's a relatively new drug that's used to treat Martian Radiation Syndrome. Therapeutic in small doses, but lethal in larger doses administered over time."

"How much time?" said Smithers-Watson.

"It would take about a month to build to full lethality."

"And where would someone get that?"

"The easiest place would be the Mars Return Clinic at the Mars Terminal. They pretty much hand it out like candy, so people can treat the symptoms when they first appear."

Morgan puffed out a long breath. "Great, so now we have to include anyone returning from Mars?"

"Not really," said Polk. "The poison was in his system, but it didn't kill him."

"But someone was trying," said Grave. "And I want to know who that is."

"We could be talking about the same person, too," said Charlize. "Maybe the killer grew impatient and opted to end Fontaine sooner."

"Or it could be two people," said Loblolly.

"Right," said Snoot. "But in any case, I agree with Grave. We need to follow up on this."

Morgan nodded. "Agreed." He turned to Polk. "Anything else, Jeremy?"

Polk shook his head. "No, that's it. Maybe more tomorrow."

"Great," said Morgan. "Okay, head on out. Let's get this guy."

Everyone resumed their march to the door.

"Except for you, Grave. I need to talk to you."

Grave stopped and waited for everyone else to clear out of the room. "Okay, what? Is this about me and Loblolly? If it is, just let me say—"

Morgan cut him off. "No, it's about you."

"Me?"

"Yes, and that damned British accent of yours."

Grave dropped his chin to his chest, one thought and one thought only on his mind. *"Shite!"*

23

Grave couldn't believe he had agreed to bring Detective Morgan Freeman along home with him, but Freeman had been persistent. He wanted to be brought up to speed on Grave's preliminary interviews with Lola LaFarge and her brother, Frankie Fontaine. All Grave wanted to do was go home, have a glass or two of Duct Tape Chardonnay, and go to bed, hoping sleep would cure him of an unwanted and persistent British accent.

Unlike most of the passengers he transported in his Austin Healey Sprite, Freeman seemed delighted with the gospel music, and like Grave, was disappointed when the car pulled into Grave's parking spot at his lighthouse home.

"That was quite amazing, sir," said Freeman. "Gospel music is embedded in my programming, but I had never really noticed it until today. I must say, it was quite delightful. The rhythms, the melodies, the passion."

"Yes," said Grave, "and loud."

Freeman laughed. "Indeed, sir, but no problem for a simdroid. I just adjusted the volume. Tell me, why do you keep it so loud?"

Everyone asked that question. "Contrary to what you might think or expect, the loud music helps me think."

"Really, how odd."

Grave raised an eyebrow. "Um, thank you."

Freeman could tell he had said the wrong thing. "No, I didn't mean—"

"No problem. Come on, let's go inside."

Freeman didn't move. "One thing before we go in."

"Yes?"

"I couldn't help notice the British accent."

Grave sighed. "It's a recurring thing, although it hadn't happened for years until now."

"So why—"

"My therapist said it was an expression and manifestation of my basic insecurities."

Freeman frowned. "Insecurities? Why, sir, I've always thought of you as supremely confident."

"Thank you, Freeman."

"Call me Morgan, sir. If we're to be partners on this investigation, we should not be so formal."

"All right, um, Morgan. And you can call me Simon, at least when we're alone. Other than that, it's Grave and Freeman, all right?"

"Yes, sir."

"And stop the sir business."

"Yes, um, *Simon.*"

"Good, good, let's go in, then." Grave glanced at the hovercar parked next to the Sprite. "I see my father and his fiancé are here, so this evening will be an eye-opener for you in many ways."

"How so, Simon?"

"Oh, I'll let you see for yourself."

They started to go in, but Grave stopped. "Wait, I want you to do something for me. If I'm ever to lick this British accent thing, I'll need your help."

"My help? But how?"

"Once we're inside, if I start to sound British, I want you to put a finger to your nose."

"Ah, I see. A signal."

"Yes, it will help me recognize the problem."

"Very well, Simon."

"And keep your finger there until I sound more American."

"Right."

"Good."

Grave took the final steps to the front door, opened it, and walked in. Freeman followed, but seeing what he saw, stopped at the door and took a step back.

24

Loblolly couldn't contain herself. "The bastard, the bastard!" she said, for about the tenth time, although this time, after too many drinks, *bastard* came out *bashtard*.

Her detective partner and good friend, Amanda Snoot, had been reduced to just nodding. Loblolly had controlled the conversation since she had arrived at Le Crabe Bleu's outdoor dining area, their favorite watering hole. While Snoot wanted to talk about her feelings for a suspect, Harry Smite, president of Save the Grapes, Loblolly continued to talk over her. Their drones, Midnight and Sparky, whirled above them in a murmuration of customers' drones above the restaurant. Such coordinated drone flights had become a new thing wherever large crowds gathered. The murmuration gave the drones something to do while their owners were occupied, and also provided entertainment for the owners below.

"And another thing, Mandy," said Loblolly. "The idiot spoke with a British accent from the moment his eyes locked on that bitch."

Amanda sighed. "Don't call me Mandy, Polly. You know I hate that."

Loblolly looked confused. "I did? I would never do that, Mandy."

Snoot rolled her eyes and then raised a hand, trying to get the attention of the waiter.

"What are you doing?" said Loblolly, trying to follow the motion of Snoot's hand.

"Getting the check," said Snoot. "I think you've had about enough for one night."

"Me? No, I've had—what?—two drinks?"

Snoot attempted a sardonic chuckle. "Oh, that second drink came about an hour ago. You're on your fifth, dear, and that's about four beyond your capacity."

"Fifth?" The word came out "fitsh," which made her laugh. "Ha! I said fitsh when I meant to say fitsh."

Snoot finally spotted the waiter, giving him an air checkmark to indicate she wanted the check. He nodded back and then disappeared inside. "Okay, check's on the way."

Loblolly looked around, but saw no sign of the waiter. "Where is he? I need another drinkie."

"No. Time to get you home, honey. We have an early morning coming up."

Loblolly sighed. "Right, right—you're right. But why are we questioning your new boyfriend?"

Snoot rapped her knuckles on the table. "Not my boyfriend. He's a suspect."

"But you said—"

"Yes, I know what I said. If we had met under different circumstances, maybe he would be boyfriend material."

Loblolly began laughing.

"Is that funny to you?"

Loblolly waived her hand back and forth. "No, no, I was just thinking about the phrase *under different circumstances*."

"What? I don't get it."

"Every time I hear that, I imagine a *circumstance* as a physical structure, like an overhang or something."

Snoot raised an eyebrow and looked around for the waiter again. "Where is that man?"

"So when someone says, 'I wouldn't do that under any circumstances,' I wonder why those structures are so off limits."

Snoot saw the waiter coming and lifted her credit card in the air to speed up the process. The waiter scanned the card, which announced, perhaps too loudly, "Seven chardonnays, one crab popover, seventy-three credits plus twelve-credit tip. Thank you!"

Snoot waited until the waiter moved away before speaking again. "Well, I for one wouldn't like to repeat this evening under any circumstances."

Loblolly snickered as she tried to wobble to her feet. "Yesh, ignactly!"

25

Detective Morgan Freeman couldn't keep his eyes off Grave's father, Jacob. If not for the age difference, Jacob and his son would have been nearly identical. Now, though, the resemblance was more like a fresh apple and a dry, shriveled one.

Not that Jacob was the only curiosity in a lighthouse filled with curiosities. Freeman had shaken hands, or rather claws, or rather hands and claws, with Red, the simcrab scientist. He'd petted the head of Lucky the Wonder Dog, Grave's crabhound, and stared in wonder at Roderick, Grave's simdroid manservant, who was immersed in a Surround Vision performance of *Casablanca*. He'd been amazed by Horace the seagull and his witty repartee.

And then, most curious of all, he had been introduced to Ida Notion, Jacob's psychic fiancé, who had rushed at him and Grave when she spotted them.

"Simon, Simon, I've had a vision!"

Grave turned to Freeman and whispered. "She's always having visions."

She stopped in front of Freeman. "My god, you look just like Morgan Freeman."

And you look like a carnival attraction, thought Freeman. And Ida would have agreed. Although she didn't dress like a gypsy fortune teller, Freeman could easily see her donning such a costume. Her dark brown hair was pulled back into a tight bun, which emphasized her round, moonlike face and large golden eyes topped by penciled-in, inverted v-shaped brows that gave her an ever-surprised aspect. A nose that would have made an eagle proud carved her face in two, resting just above large, puffy lips painted scarlet. Her face in total seemed to be inspired by a Mr. Potato Head set. Freeman smiled at her.

"I know," said Freeman. "I'm built that way."

"Oh, oh, a simdroid. And a detective to boot, I bet."

"Yes, ma'am. A recent change in duties."

She nodded toward Grave. "Just stay close to this one. He'll teach you what to know, what to do."

Freeman nodded. "Of course."

Grave tapped her on the shoulder. "Ahem."

Ida startled. "Oh, oh yes, the vision. It was so strange." She stretched out the word.

"In what way, Ida?"

"I saw a man floating in wine. How about *that* for strange."

Freeman's eyes went wide. "And that is the very case we're working on. The murder of Mr. Falcon Fontaine, owner-vintner of a local vineyard."

Now it was Ida's turn to go wide-eyed. "Oh, my."

"I don't suppose you saw who killed him," said Grave. "That would be very helpful."

Ida shrugged. "Maybe, Simon, but as usual with my visions, the images were not all that clear."

"Blurs," said Grave.

Ida frowned. "I'm afraid so." But then she beamed. "But I can tell you this. There were two of them, the blurs, *two* murderers."

"Two?" said Freeman. "Two men?"

Ida threw up her hands. "Dunno. Could have been two women, or a man and a woman, or a man and a simdroid, or a woman and a simdroid, or two simdroids."

Grave smiled at Freeman. "As you can see, Ida can be very helpful, but not always definitive." He turned to Ida. "But you've moved the investigation forward, Ida. We now know we're looking for two people or, as you say, some mix of humans and simdroids."

"I wonder," said Freeman. "Were the murderers the same size?"

Ida put a hand to her chin, thinking. "Everything happened so fast, but let me see, let me see. Yes, all three—the victim and the two murderers—were different sizes."

"Interesting," said Grave. "Did you see how the murder unfolded?"

Ida nodded vigorously. "Oh, yes. One of the blurs—the victim, I think—was talking to another blur. And then another blur came up from behind and grabbed the victim. And then—oh, it was so horrible—the blur in front started stabbing the victim blur."

"But their relative sizes, Ida. Which blur was tallest?"

Ida went back to stroking her chin. "Tallest, tallest—oh, yes, the blur behind the victim. And the shortest blur was the murderer blur in front of the victim blur, who seemed to be midway between the two in height." She looked back and forth between them. "Does that help?"

Grave nodded. "I'm sure it will be very helpful, Ida. And if you think of anything else, please let me know."

"Oh, of course, Simon."

Jacob Grave yelled at them from the sofa. "Are we ever going to eat or are you three just going to natter on all evening?"

Grave winked at Freeman. "Welcome to my world."

26

When Grave and his drone, Barry, made their way out of the lighthouse the next morning, Detective Morgan Freeman was waiting.

"Good morning, sir," he said. "I hope you had a restful night."

Grave shook his head. "Never do when I'm on a case. Sorted facts and suspicions all night. How about you?"

"Oh, I had a good long talk with Red. His work is so important and yet he's lost funding."

"Yes, I know. So, are you ready to go?"

"Yes, but I want to talk to you about something before we have to face the gospel music."

"The British accent? Don't worry about that. We have a plan, right?

"Yes, the finger to the nose thing."

"Exactly. So, if you ever catch me doing that, just place a finger on your nose. I've worked through this problem before, and I know that will help me rid myself of this little curse."

Freeman shrugged. "As you wish, sir, but that's not what I wanted to talk about."

"Oh, what then?"

"Your relationship with Ms. LaFarge."

Grave seemed taken aback. "What about it? There really isn't a relationship anymore. We were, um, *involved* once, but that was years ago."

"Still, statistics suggest you will not be as objective as you need to be with her, particularly as it relates to her being a prime suspect in this murder."

"Prime suspect? Ridiculous!"

"Is it? Is it, sir? You know relatives are always under suspicion, right? They're the first people we look at."

"Yes, but—"

Freeman held up a hand. "I just have a suggestion."

"Oh, and what's that?"

"When it comes to Ms. LaFarge, let me take the lead. Let me do the questioning. You can be there, of course, but let me handle it."

Grave sighed. "I just don't see how this could possibly—"

Freeman rolled his eyes and tapped a finger on his nose.

Grave growled. "Shite!"

Len Boswell

27

Smithers-Watson took the call from Barry, and listened quietly as Barry described Ida Notion's vision. Every core of Smithers-Watson's processors urged him to hang up. *Visons? Nonsense!* But he listened nonetheless. Ms. Notion had a way of being at least partially right.

"Thank you, Barry," he said. "Tell Grave we'll follow up as he has instructed."

He blinked hard and the call ended.

Charlize pulled the faux Duesenberg she had built from a kit into Falcon Fontaine's reserved parking spot in front of the winery entrance. "What is it?"

"That was Barry. It seems our Ms. Notion has had another of her dubious visions."

"Oh, wonderful. I wish just once she could actually see the vision clearly."

"I know. Anyway, according to her vision, two people were involved in the killing."

"Interesting."

81

"Yes, and Grave wants us to start our interviews with an actual lineup of the suspects, to see how tall they are, in relation to our sadly dead Mr. Fontaine."

"A lineup?"

"Yes."

Charlize sighed. "Won't that just tip our hand?"

"By formally notifying them that they are in fact suspects?"

"Yes, it seems to be a premature move."

"And yet."

"And yet Grave has ordered it. I mean, we don't even know how tall Fontaine is—was."

"Actually, we do. Polk confirms that he is exactly five foot six, which also matches his driver's license."

"Okay, then. No, wait, how are we going to measure *them?*"

"Not a problem," said Smithers-Watson. "My latest upgrade included a dimensional scanner. I can measure anything, from an atom to a skyscraper, to within four ten-thousandths of a millimeter."

Charlize cocked her head. "I'll have to get me some of that."

"Yes, but it's a bit disconcerting at first. Once you turn it on, it literally measures everything within your visual range. So when we have them in a lineup, I'll also receive data on the dimensions of the room, the size of their heads, and so on. It takes concentration to focus on just the one dimension of height."

"But you can do it, right?"

"Yes, of course."

Charlize nodded. "Okay, let's go in."

Charlize got out of the Duesenberg and started walking to the front door. Smithers-Watson followed, noting that the gravel in the parking lot varied from fifteen millimeters to 1.348 centimeters.

28

The office of Save the Grapes was nothing more than a battered school desk sitting next to a dumpster outside Bob's Crab Shack. A small sign tacked onto the wall near the restaurant's employee entrance announced, "Save the Grapes, office hours vary. Please be patient."

Snoot was miffed. "He said he'd be here first thing."

Loblolly thought to answer, but the smell of the dumpster crab parts and her pounding head—why did she drink so much?—had her on the verge of throwing up. All she could get out was, "Errrrr . . ."

Snoot rolled her eyes. "You're in *great* shape, aren't you? Maybe you should just go back to the hovercruiser." She thought about the idea for a few seconds, and shook her head. "No, forget that. Just go back to the cruiser and wait outside. Can't have you ruining the cruiser."

Loblolly waved her off. "No, I'll be fine, but maybe you can do the questioning."

Snoot nodded.

"And don't forget to measure him. Grave was very insistent about that."

Snoot looked up at her drone, Midnight, who was whirling in circles with Loblolly's new drone, Sparky. "Don't worry. I've already told Midnight to scan him. Harry won't even know he's being scanned."

"Harry?"

Snoot blushed. "I mean Mr. Smite."

Loblolly cocked her head. "You like him, don't you?"

"Don't be silly."

"No, no, you're blushing even more."

Snoot huffed. "Okay, okay, I'm attracted to him."

Loblolly shrugged. "No biggie. Fine with me, but are you sure you can be objective here?" She turned and looked down the alley to the street, and saw no Harry Smite. "I mean if he ever shows up."

"I'll be fine. Besides, we can't have you throwing up on his shoes in the middle of questioning."

Loblolly attempted a laugh, but pain shot through her temples. "Oh, god, ouch. A fair point, Mandy."

Snoot let the unwanted "Mandy" go and nodded her head toward the street. "Okay, here he comes."

29

Grave parked the Sprite in front of the Fontaine Mansion, and he and Freeman climbed out.

"Remember," said Grave. "A finger to your nose if I lapse into a British accent."

"And that will work?"

Grave nodded. "Oh, yes. Immediate feedback, like a finger to a nose, helps me recognize what's happening. Then I can control it. It's a trick my therapist taught me. I think he called it a feedback loop." He frowned. "Or maybe not. Maybe another term. Not important. Anyway, let's go."

Freeman shrugged. "Okay, but let me question Lola."

Grave nodded. "Fine, I'll take Frankie." He looked around for Barry. "Where's that drone of mine?"

Freeman pointed behind Grave. Barry was hovering there, just above Grave's head.

"Here, sir," said Barry.

"Measure Lola when she comes to the door."

"No problem," said Barry. "But I doubt that she's grown since I last saw her. She's five foot two, and you know that."

Grave huffed. "I know that, but we have to be professional here. Measure her again and then stay outside and wait."

"But how will I measure the brother?"

"No problem," said Freeman. "I have scanning abilities."

"Then why don't you scan Lola, too. It would seem to be a more objective measurement."

Freeman nodded. "Let's both measure her; then we can compare results."

"Yes," said Barry, "that sounds good."

"Are you two finished?" said Grave. "I'd like to get this over with."

Freeman nodded and Barry wobbled in the affirmative.

"Okay, then," said Grave. "Let's do this."

They approached the glass door, and peered through it. Lola had apparently been expecting them, because they could see her walking toward the door. Grave tried his best not to gasp. She looked like she had been poured into her skin-tight black vinyl leggings, and her pink blouse was open three buttons down, revealing the wonder of her décolletage.

Grave whispered to Barry and Freeman. "Prepare to scan."

Neither replied as Lola opened the door and smiled at them. "Welcome back, Grave." She looked at Freeman. "And who do we have here?"

Freeman reached out his hand. "Detective Morgan Freeman, ma'am."

She cocked her head. "You're a simdroid, aren't you?"

Freeman nodded. "Yes, ma'am. Helping Detective Grave with the case. And please accept my condolences for your loss."

She said nothing, and turned back to Grave. "Come in, then. Frankie is in the library." She glanced at her watch. "I hope this won't take too long. I'm meeting with my father's lawyer about the reading of the will. He should be here shortly, and I'd prefer that be a private meeting between him and Frankie and me."

"Noted," said Grave. "Although, perhaps we can arrange to meet with him at another time."

Lola squinted at him. "Always working, aren't you?" said Lola. "Let me guess. *Inheritance is a motive for murder*. Am I right?"

"It can be, although we have come to no conclusion in that regard."

"Good, because the only conclusion is that neither I nor Frankie was motivated to kill our father. We had our differences, of course, but no, that would never lead to murder."

"Of course not," said Grave. "Shall we resume our conversation, then?"

Lola took a step back and motioned them in. "Absolutely. This way, gentlemen."

Grave and Freeman followed, trailed by Barry, who had already conducted his scan. Ms. Lola LaFarge was in fact five-two, plus or minus a millimeter or two.

Grave had also begun a scan, but it was focused entirely on Lola's behind as she led them down the glass hallways to the library.

30

Loblolly watched Harry Smite walking toward them and couldn't help noticing that he checked every box when it came to Snoot's preferences in men.

Height, short, so she could look directly in his eyes. Eyes, blue, because they made her weak in the knees. Hair, brown and unruly—she didn't want a man who pampered himself or spent time looking in mirrors. Confident, check—you could tell by his swagger. Smile, broad, quick, and disarming. Body, thin but not emaciated. Muscles, just enough to get by. Last name, one syllable—she would never take a man's last name in the event of marriage. The best she'd do is hyphenate her own name, and Snoot-Smite was just the sort of married name that might work for her.

Loblolly nodded at her drone, Sparky, who flew toward Smite, scanning his height as he came. Smite's own drone, a noisy old model with propellers, moved to block Sparky, but she was too quick for him.

Smite swatted at Sparky. "What's with your drone?"

Loblolly shrugged. "Just eager to meet yours, I guess. What's its name?"

Smite pointed at it. "Defiance."

Snoot, who had been silently tracking Smite, chuckled. "That sounds perfect for you. Considering our last run-in."

Smite held his arms out. "Look at me. No knife. I've learned my lesson."

"Have you?"

He smiled at her. "If you're here to arrest me, I guess not."

Loblolly cleared her throat, a signal to Snoot that she was taking over from this point. They'd agreed that Snoot was not as objective as she should be about Smite, so Loblolly should lead the interrogation. "We're not here to arrest you."

"Well, that's a relief."

"But we do have questions."

Smite nodded. "As well you should. But do you mind if I sit down?" He pointed at the school desk next to the dumpster. "In my office chair."

Snoot snickered. "By all means."

Smite walked over and sat down. "Good to get off my feet. Protesting is an exhausting business."

"I bet," said Loblolly. "Comfy now?"

Smite smiled at her. "Very."

Loblolly nodded. "Then let us begin."

31

Charlize and Smithers-Watson walked slowly down the line of Château de Crabe Rouge employees that Fontaine's executive secretary, Blanche LaTour, had hurriedly assembled. Some employees smiled at them, others glowered, and still others, surprised by the detectives' nineteenth-century clothing, chuckled and elbowed the next person in line as if to say, "Get a load of this."

Charlize didn't care how they looked at her. She was looking at them for any sign of anxiety. Would they become nervous on her approach? Would they meet her eyes or look away?

Most just nodded as she passed, unconcerned by her and thankful for a break in the workday. The people she had already interviewed, however—Art Travis Tee, Angus McBride, Nigel Forthwith III, and even Blanche LaTour—offered only frowns and nervous twitches, not happy at all that she and Smithers-Watson had returned for further questioning.

Smithers-Watson moved down the line behind Charlize, recording each employee's reaction and scanning them for height. His software was already loading the data into a program that would sort through the various combinations and permutations of employees to identify likely matches for the murderous duo.

Finally, they reached the end of the line, and Charlize turned back to face them. "Thank you very much for taking time away from your duties to meet with us. I will have questions for some of you, including several people we've already talked with, over the next few hours. You may all return to your duties now; if we choose to talk with you, your Ms. LaTour will let you know." She scanned the line of people, looking for any negative reaction, and saw none. "Again, thank you for your time."

Ms. LaTour stepped out of the line and turned to face the other employees. "Okay, that's it. You may return to your jobs. Oh, and one final thing. Please record this quarter hour on your timesheets as administrative time. Okay, we're done here."

As the employees dispersed, LaTour walked over to Charlize and Smithers-Watson. "I've set you up in the break room again. If you need anything further from me, I'll be back in my office in the executive suite."

Charlize smiled at her. "Actually, we'd like to talk with you again."

LaTour raised an eyebrow. "Really? Now?"

Charlize nodded. "Yes, just a couple of questions."

LaTour sighed. "The break room?"

"Yes," said Charlize. "That will do nicely."

"Come along, then," said LaTour, turning away from them and walking away.

Charlize waited until she was several steps away, and turned to Smithers-Watson. "Did you get what you needed?"

"Yes, definitely. The heights vary from five-two to six-eight, as well as an outlier for that Bacchus simdroid, who's a whopping seven-ten."

"Keep him in the mix, as well as the other simdroids."

"Very well. So, we're starting with LaTour?"

"Yes, and she's in the tall group. A little over five-ten."

Charlize looked over at LaTour, who had stopped and turned back, wondering why Charlize wasn't following. "Okay, let's do this."

They began walking toward LaTour, who gave them a frown and turned on her heels, heading for the break room again.

32

If a man can be said to be the epitome of boredom, Frankie Fontaine was giving it his best shot. Every question was met with a yawn or a glance at his watch or a look away or an outright refusal to answer.

"We can do this down at the station if you like," said Grave.

Another yawn from Frankie, and another nose tap from Freeman, who seemed unable to get Grave's attention.

"You realize you're making yourself a prime suspect by this behavior," said Grave.

Frankie rolled his eyes. "As if."

Freeman cleared his throat and tapped his nose twice.

"Well, not very helpful," said Grave, "but it's good to hear your voice."

Frankie looked at his watch again as Freeman cleared his throat even louder and tapped a finger to his nose.

Grave turned to Freeman. "Cuff him."

Freeman tapped his nose, but Grave missed the signal again.

Lola put herself between Freeman and her brother. "No, don't you dare." She turned to Grave. "I told you. He was here with me at the time of the murder."

Freeman, unable to get Grave's attention, pointed his finger at Lola. "Or you're giving each other an alibi."

Lola seemed stunned. "Me? What nonsense. We were here, both of us. And neither of us wanted him dead."

Freeman pressed her. "Can anyone else confirm that you were here? A servant perhaps?"

Lola sneered at him. "I've already told you, *detective*, the servants had the evening off—we do that from time to time."

"Sounds convenient to me," said Freeman.

Grave turned back to Frankie. "I need to hear it from your lips. Otherwise, I'm going to take you in."

"Say it," said Lola.

Frankie rolled his eyes. "Oh, very well. I was here at the time of the murder, detective, as my sister can attest and verify."

Grave nodded. "Good. Now, let's move on. We'd like to talk with all the servants."

"But why?" said Lola. "I've already told you they had the night off."

"Then they'll have little to tell us, which will have us on our way in no time."

Lola shook her head in disbelief. "Well, if you must, but this is so ridiculous, Simon."

"As I've said, it won't take long, Lola. We simply have to verify what you've told us."

"And your servants may have some insight into the crime," said Freeman.

Lola shook her head, and sighed. "All right, all right. Do you want them all at once, or one at a time?"

"Both," said Grave. "All at once, then one at a time."

"A suggestion," she said.

"Oh? What?"

"Ditch the British accent. It will just confuse them."

Grave shot a glance at Freeman, who shot a finger into his nostril.

33

Harry Smite sat squeezed into his school desk next to the dumpster as Snoot and Loblolly paced back and forth in front of him, asking questions. Their drones, Midnight and Sparky, hovered nearby, along with Smite's drone, Defiance.

"So you were in the parking lot at the time of the murder?" said Loblolly.

Smite shrugged. "So it seems. I'm usually there from early in the day till about seven or so in the evening."

"That's a long day," said Snoot. *Oh, those eyes of his,* she thought. *Like the proverbial deep pools of blue.*

"But necessary."

"And why is that?" said Loblolly. *His eyes are so shifty,* she thought. *He has to be hiding something.*

He smiled at them. "It's a two-fer. In the morning, I can talk to the night shift as they leave, and in the evening, I can talk to the day shift as they leave."

"Of course, of course," said Snoot. *Oh, that smile,* she thought. *Hold me up, somebody, my knees are buckling.*

"And what do you talk to them about?" said Loblolly. *I'd like to slap that sly smile off his face*, she thought. *Right now.*

"About grapes, of course," he said. "About using grapes to make the wine, not chemicals and nanobots." He screwed up his face. "It's disgusting."

"And on the evening in question, who did you talk to?" said Loblolly.

He ran a hand through his hair. "No one in particular. It's more like shouting at them as they head for their hovercars."

"And did anyone stop to talk?" said Snoot. *That hair, those hands*, she thought. *Like twin miracles.*

He laughed. "Stop? No, never. They usually just pick up the pace." He laughed again. "I seem to have that effect on people. I speed them up, get them to their cars quicker."

God, I hate that laugh, thought Loblolly. *Beyond sardonic.*

God, I love that laugh, thought Snoot. *So engaging. So alive. Such joie de vivre!*

Smite looked back and forth at them. One looked like she wanted to tear him apart, and the other one seemed to be daydreaming about something pleasant. "So, is that it?"

"No," said Loblolly. "On that particular evening, did anything about the shift change seem unusual?"

"Like what?"

"People perhaps moving faster than usual? Acting strange? Anything?"

He shook his head, then stopped. "Wait, there was one thing."

"Oh?" said Loblolly.

Oh, oh, thought Snoot. *He's so cute.*

"Yes, it just came to me. The limousine."

"Limousine?" said Loblolly.

"Fontaine's, I'm sure. Picks him up most evenings, to take him home or take him to the airport or the Mars Terminal."

"The Mars Terminal?"

"Yeah, he's trying to introduce his nanobot-contrived wines on Mars, I hear. Disgusting."

"But there would be no Fontaine to pick up that night," said Snoot.

"Right, but that's why I just remembered it. The limo picked up two people I'd never seen before, and then sped away."

Loblolly's eyes went wide. "Can you describe them?"

"Yes, a little. There was a woman, pretty and petite, and a man in a gray suit, much taller than the woman."

"Anything else?"

"No, they were running, so I didn't have much time to study them."

Bingo, thought Loblolly. *Must be that LaFarge bitch.*

Oh, oh, thought Snoot. *I could just eat him up.*

34

Blanche LaTour crossed and uncrossed her legs with every question, and glanced at the break room clock after each answer.

"Are you late for something?" said Charlize.

LaTour crossed and uncrossed her legs. "No, why do you ask?" she said, glancing at the clock.

"You keep glancing at the clock."

She shrugged. "There's a lot to do now that Mr. Fontaine is dead. We need to keep things going, stay on schedule. A lot of that burden falls on me."

Charlize nodded. "Understood. I think we have all we need from you for the moment, Ms. LaTour." She glanced at Smithers-Watson, who was shaking his head. "You have another question?"

"Yes, just one. Do you have CCTV cameras here?"

LaTour crossed and uncrossed her legs. "Yes, six on the outside, one at each corner of the building, plus one at the front entrance and one at the docks out back." She tried to not glance at the clock but did anyway.

"And what about inside?"

She crossed and uncrossed her legs. "Um, I know we have one in the visitor greeting area and one in the tasting area, but other than that, um, I'm not sure." She shot a look at the clock. "So, is that it?"

"We'd like to see those CCTV tapes. Do you have a head of security?"

LaTour crossed and uncrossed her legs. "Yes, George Gitt." She glanced at the clock. "I can send him in if you like."

Charlize shook her head. "No, it would be better if you take us to him. I'm assuming he has the necessary equipment for viewing the tapes?"

LaTour wasn't sure if they had asked a question, so she kept her legs crossed.

"That was a question, Ms. LaTour," said Charlize.

"Oh," said LaTour, crossing and uncrossing her legs. "Yes, of course."

She glanced at the clock and then stood. "Shall we?"

35

The cook, the butler, the manservant, the part-time gardener, the chauffer, and the three housemaids all confirmed that they had been given the evening off, commencing precisely at 7:00 p.m. on the evening of the murder.

Because all of them were simdroids and because all simdroids are programmed to tell the truth, the group interview was brief. After scanning them for height, Grave and Freeman began the questioning.

Did you have the evening off? All said yes.

When were you told you could have the evening off? All said that morning, at the staff meeting.

When did you actually leave the mansion or retire to your quarters? Here the answers varied. The cook, a Julia Child model, had left first, at 6:00 p.m., after delivering a tray of sandwiches and drinks to the library for Lola and Frankie, who had told her she could leave right away. The chauffer, a Jimmy Stewart model, had left next, at 6:15 p.m., to pick up Mr. Fontaine, as usual. The gardener, a George Bush model from the popular presidential line, had left at 5:00 p.m., his usual quitting time. The manservant, a Tony Curtis model, had retired to his quarters at 6:50, after laying out Mr. Fontaine's evening clothes. The butler, who like

Freeman was a Morgan Freeman model, had had the last contact with Lola and Frankie. He had knocked on the door to the library, as he always did before entering any closed room, but had not entered because "they seemed to be having an argument." He had opted to leave them to it, and had retired to his quarters precisely at 7:00 p.m., after sending the three housemaids, all Marilyn Monroe models, on their way.

Grave had then dismissed all the servants except the Butler and the Chauffer, who gave each other confused looks, wondering why they had not been dismissed with the others.

"Don't worry," said Grave. "Just a brief follow-up question or two for each of you."

Neither looked relieved.

"If you like, we can meet privately with each of you, or we can just ask the questions now."

Both shrugged.

"All right, we'll do it now." Grave turned to the chauffer. "Do they call you Jimmy?"

"No, sir. My name is Speedy."

"Really?"

"Mr. Fontaine's idea. He likes me to drive fast."

"I see. So, when you got to the winery that evening, what did you do?"

"I parked out front, as usual."

"And when he didn't show up, what did you do?"

"I called Ms. LaTour to see if he had been delayed."

"And?"

"She said he was inspecting a fermentation tank, and that I should wait."

"And how long did you wait?"

"I didn't. I explained that I had the evening off and would really like to leave."

"So . . ."

"So, she said for me to put the limo into auto mode and be on my way."

"You left? When?"

"Just before seven, maybe five of."

"And how did you leave?"

"In a driverless hovercab."

"And it came that fast?"

"Was already there, but whoever had called it, hadn't shown up."

"Odd."

"I guess."

Grave gave Speedy a nod. "Thank you, um, Speedy. You can go now."

Speedy smiled and speedily left the room as Grave turned to the Butler. "So, um, what's your name?"

The butler shrugged. "Alex Cross."

Grave chuckled. "So, let me guess. Mr. Fontaine was a fan of those movies?"

"Yes."

Freeman, who had been silent for some time, chimed in. "Then why are you not dressed like Alex Cross?"

Cross looked down at his tuxedo. "Mr. Fontaine insisted on it. I think of it as a disguise."

"Let me get to the questions," said Grave. "You said you knocked on the door to the library at precisely 7:00 p.m.?"

"Yes, there's a clock in the hallway, so it's pretty easy to be precise. And I'm a simdroid, after all, keeping precise track of time is built in."

"Yes, of course," said Grave. "So, you said they were having an argument. What about?"

Cross shook his head. "I really don't know. All I can tell you is what I heard during the few seconds after the knock Or rather, both knocks."

"All right, what?"

Cross cleared his throat and began repeating the fragment of the argument, in the voices of Frankie and Lola.

LOLA (shouting): It's over. Over!

FRANKIE (louder): Not by a long shot!

"And then I knocked again."

FRANKIE: Whoever you are, go away!

LOLA: *Go!*

"And then I turned on my heels and left them to it."

"That's it?" said Grave. "Nothing more?"

Cross shook his head. "I'm sorry."

"Had you ever heard them arguing before?" said Freeman.

"No."

"Or since?" said Grave.

"No."

Grave sighed. "Okay, thank you for your time, Alex."

"Yes, sir. May I go now?"

Grave nodded. "Of course. Oh, and could you send in Ms. LaFarge on your way out?"

"Of course, sir." He stood and left the room, leaving Grave and Freeman to themselves.

"So, what do you think?" said Grave.

Freeman shrugged. "I think I'd look good in a tux."

Grave laughed. "No, I meant—"

There was a knock at the door, and then Lola LaFarge stuck her head in. "Safe to come into the interrogation room?"

Grave couldn't help smiling at her. "Yes, but has your lawyer arrived?"

Lola stepped all the way into the room. "He's talking with Frankie at the moment, but if you're ready, I can go get him for you."

"That would be wonderful."

She smiled at him and left the room.

Grave turned back to Freeman. "So seriously, what do you think?"

"The butler seems to have confirmed their alibi."

Grave nodded. "So it seems, but I'm still wondering about that argument."

"Probably nothing. Sibling stuff."

"Yes, probably."

There was a knock on the door.

36

George Gitt, head of security at Château de Crabe Rouge, popped a mint into his mouth and pointed at the array of monitors showing interior and exterior views of the building.

"Here at the Shat-toe duh Crab Roogie we pride ourselves on security. We have to protect our formulas, you see. International espionage, you see. Perhaps even interplanetary, what with Mars in the mix now. Our Mr. Fontaine's been trying to get a foothold there, don't you know. Of course, that might not be possible now. I mean what with his death."

Charlize wasn't sure what to make of the man sitting between her and Smithers-Watson. He was a large man, well beyond obese, as his poor, squeaking chair could testify. His head was like a bowling ball covered in wattles and dewlaps that shook and shivered as he spoke. His eyes were beady blue and set close above a mushroom of a nose, which itself sat above razor-thin lips and a receding chin.

"So," began Charlize. "About your CCTV system. Do your cameras cover every area of the facility?"

"Normally, yes."

"Normally? What do you mean?"

"I mean they normally do, but the past month or so, we've been changing them out for new ones." He slapped his hand on the control panel. "Look up there at Monitor Seven. And then look at Monitor Twelve. See the difference?"

Charlize nodded. "Twelve clearly has better definition and black-white contrast."

Gitt beamed at her. "I picked them out myself. And had to defend my selection with Mr. Fontaine himself."

"Interesting," said Smithers-Watson. "So, back to the monitors. How many are down at any given time, for these switch-outs of yours?"

"Ah," said Gitt, "an interesting point. Only one camera a day has been affected, and that one for only the half hour or so it takes for the technician to make the switch."

"What about the camera covering the fermentation tank where Mr. Fontaine was killed?" said Charlize.

"That would be Monitor Four, and as you can see, it has been switched out for the new camera. Wonderful definition, you see."

"Yes, but when was it switched out?"

Gitt fumbled for a clipboard hanging from the console. "Let me see here. Oh, oh my goodness. It appears to have been switched out the other evening, towards the end of the day shift."

"The evening Mr. Fontaine was killed?"

"Yes."

"So the camera was offline for half an hour?" said Smithers-Watson.

"Um, probably longer, it being the end of the day. The technician could have taken the camera off line and then left for the day. Overtime is strictly forbidden here."

"Okay, Mr. Gitt," said Charlize. "Show us what you've got on tape for that evening."

Gitt nodded and began punching buttons with his fat fingers. "Should be right about here." He tapped one final button with a flourish and the tape began to roll.

Mr. Fontaine, looking none too happy, could be seen walking up to the fermentation tank.

And then the tape went black for a few seconds. When it resumed, it showed police officers stringing crime scene tape over the entire area.

Smithers-Watson summed up the situation: "Damn!"

37

Jacob "Jake" Dilby, the Fontaine family's attorney, entered the library with a broad smile and an already stretched out hand, his grip causing Grave to wince with pain while returning a smile he hoped would successfully counter Dilby's gleaming choppers.

He was a tall man, about an inch taller than Grave, and square-jawed handsome. His firm grip matched a body that suggested he was a gym rat when he wasn't clocking billable hours. Grave guessed his age as mid-thirties, maybe forty, tops. His blond hair was cut short, almost a buzz cut, and drew attention to his face, which was baby-bottom smooth except for crow's feet around his dark brown eyes. His nose looked like it had been carved by a master, and twitched left and right as he spoke.

"Jacob Dilby, attorney-at-law, but you can call me Jake, everyone does. I heard from Lola that you might have questions." He looked at his watch and shook his head. "Time flies. I can give you five minutes, six tops."

Grave raised an eyebrow. "You'll give us every minute we need to satisfy our questions, Mr. Dilby."

Dilby sighed. "Well, let's get to it, then. I'm on the clock."

Grave nodded in the direction of Freeman. "This is my partner, Detective Freeman."

Dilby nodded at Freeman and smiled. "A simdroid, right? Morgan Freeman model? God, I loved that man. Great actor. Always delivered."

"Yes," said Freeman, frowning.

"All right, then," said Grave. "Have a seat, Mr. Dilby, and I'll try to keep this first meeting brief."

Dilby sat down in a wing chair opposite Grave and Freeman, who sat down on a leather couch.

"First meeting? What do you mean?"

"Nothing bad," said Grave. "But sometimes we feel the need to follow up with witnesses after our first discussions."

"Witness? I'm not a witness. I was miles away when poor Falcon was killed."

"No, not a witness," said Grave. "But someone who might have a valuable contribution to make to our investigation."

Dilby nodded, satisfied. "So, you have questions?"

"You said you were miles away. Where exactly?"

"My office, city center, on the square."

"And I assume you have someone who can verify that?"

Dilby shrugged. "My secretary."

"Good. Now, apart from your whereabouts, how did you hear about the murder?"

"From his son, Frankie, that same evening."

"Do you remember a more precise time?"

Dilby looked at the ceiling, thinking. "Um, I think it was at eight or thereabouts. He wanted to know about the will."

"Who would inherit and how much?"

"Yes."

"And what did you tell him?"

"Nothing, I can only do that at the official release of the will."

"But being the son, he stood to inherit?"

Dilby rolled his eyes. "I think it's safe to say that several people stood to inherit."

"And that list would include Lola LaFarge as well, I assume."

Dilby frowned. "No, absolutely not. They had been estranged for many years, you see, and only recently made amends. There was talk of a codicil to include her, but that never made it past the draft stages. A shame, really, she would have shared equally with Frankie on the bulk of the assets had it gone through."

"Interesting," said Grave. "And was she aware of this?"

"No, I held that strictly confidential."

"Okay, so you mentioned the *bulk* of the assets. Are others included in the will?"

"Yes, another twenty people or so. Mr. Fontaine was a taskmaster, and not widely liked, but he always rewarded good work."

"So, we're talking about employees?"

"Yes, small shares in the winery."

"And were these people aware of their potential inheritance?"

Dilby shrugged. "That I can't say. Best to ask them. But can you wait a day or so? I need to formally notify them of the reading of the will. Time, place, etcetera."

Grave smiled at him. "I guess I can live with a one-day delay, but no more. In fact, when the notices go out, I want to be copied." He leveled his gaze on Dilby. "Do we understand each other?"

Dilby nodded, then stood, his arm shooting out again. Grave neither stood nor offered his hand in response.

Dilby pulled back his hand. "Well, then." He smiled at Grave, nodded at Freeman, and strode out of the room.

Grave turned to Freeman. "So, what do you think?"

"I think things just got complicated."

"Indeed," said Grave. "Indeed."

38

Loblolly and Snoot took their time heading back to the station. They knew Grave and Freeman and Charlize and Smithers-Watson would require more time to interview witnesses and suspects. Loblolly set the hovercruiser on autopilot and sank back in her seat, closing her eyes as it picked up speed and merged onto the highway. Even at the posted speed limits, it would take over twenty minutes to get to the station.

She turned to Snoot, who seemed to be in some kind of dream state. "What's up with you?"

Snoot just stared out the window, a smile on her face.

"Amanda, I'm talking to you."

Snoot startled. "What? What did you say?"

"You. What's up with you?"

"I think I may be in love, or at least extreme like."

Loblolly gave her a look of disbelief. "Wait, you mean that weasel Smite?"

Snoot frowned. "Weasel? No, I think he's nice and really sweet."

Loblolly raised her eyebrows. "Crushin' on him, are you? Jeez, that's bizarre."

"Careful, girl, or I'll make fun of your bizarre crush on Grave."

Loblolly winced. "Ouch and touché to that. Fortunately, I think I may be coming out of that fog. That Lola person still has her hooks in him, and he's doing nothing to resist."

"Sorry about that, Polly."

Loblolly let out a long sigh. "Anyway, enough about men. Were you able to reach Charlize?"

"Yeah, they were with the security guy, so the timing was perfect. They'll be looking at the footage from the exterior CCTV cameras to see if they can get a better view of the people running to the limo."

"Good, and I hope it's that Lola bitch. I'd like to take her down, lock her up, and throw away the key."

Snoot just smiled at her.

"What?" said Loblolly. "What's that look about?"

Snoot continued smiling. "I guess we're back on men again."

39

When Smithers-Watson received the call from Detective Snoot, he and Charlize were already heading out of the security room after wrapping up their conversation and review of CCTV footage with George Gitt.

"Wait," said Smithers-Watson. "That was Snoot. She wants us to look at one more tape."

Gitt, who was shaking Charlize's hand, turned and gave Smithers-Watson a look equal parts puzzlement, irritation, and frustration. "What, another one?"

"Let me guess," said Charlize. "The entrance to this building, which is also one of the exits."

"Exactly," said Smithers-Watson. "The front entrance."

"I should have thought of it myself." She turned to Gitt. "Sir, we'll take a look at the tapes for all entrances and exits."

Gitt rolled his eyes. "Now?"

"Yes, of course," said Charlize.

Gitt nodded and motioned them back into the viewing room. "That would be twelve cameras in all."

"One entrance on each side of the building, each covered by three cameras, one above the door and one on either corner, to give us three different perspectives."

Gitt's eyes went wide. "How could you know that?"

She smiled back at him and raised a finger into the air. "Elementary!"

Simon Grave and the Wrath of Grapes

40

The meeting was raucous, everyone trying to make their point.

"It's Lola LaFarge and a tall man," shouted Loblolly, sneering at Grave. "We have a witness who saw them racing to get into Fontaine's limo just minutes after Fontaine was killed."

"Maybe," said Charlize. "The CCTV tapes show *a* man and *a* woman getting into *a* limo, but there were actually three limos, and everyone seemed to be rushing to get into them, like they were late. Maybe they had a flight to catch."

Grave shot a look at Loblolly. "But the fact is, Lola LaFarge has a rock-solid alibi. The butler confirmed that Lola and her brother were in Fontaine's library, having an argument, at the time of the crime."

"What about that other suspect, Nigel Forthwith the Third? Did anyone interview him?" said Captain Morgan.

"Yes," said Charlize, "and he, too, seems to have a rock-solid alibi. In fact, everyone at the winery seems to have an alibi. Maybe what we're looking at is a conspiracy to commit murder."

Grave nodded. "That would fit what we learned from the family lawyer. Pretty much everyone is in for a piece of the estate."

114

Simon Grave and the Wrath of Grapes

"I still think it's Lola LaFarge," said Loblolly, giving Grave another harsh look.

Grave rolled his eyes and huffed. "I *said* she has an alibi. It's not her."

"Is to," shouted Loblolly. "You're not being objective."

"And you are?"

Captain Morgan raised his arms and his voice. "Stop it, both of you."

He looked back and forth between them until he could see they had both calmed down. "Now, let me make a suggestion, if I may."

Everyone nodded.

"We have the CCTV tapes, correct?"

"Yes, I downloaded them all," said Smithers-Watson.

"And I also assume we have scans of all the prime suspects."

Everyone nodded.

"So, then," said Morgan "Let's do two things. First, let's deal with the murder as seen by our psychic Ida Notion. We've been assuming her vision is correct, right? So let's put all the scans into a scanimation sequence, matching up all the possible combinations and permutations of suspects, tall and short. Then, we'll bring Ida in and see if she can identify our murderers."

"Wow, that sounds great," said Grave.

Morgan smiled at him. "Two, let's take the scans of the workers at the winery and using the CCTV tapes and recognition software, identify where each and every one of them was at the time of the murder."

"Yes, yes," said Charlize. "And by elimination, we should be able to identify anyone not an employee—even who got into those limos."

"Precisely," said Smithers-Watson.

Freeman stepped forward. "Captain, I have experience with scanimation and would like to take the lead on that."

"Good," said Morgan. "And Smithers-Watson, if you could take the lead on the CCTV work."

Smithers-Watson nodded.

"Okay, then," said Morgan. "Let's get to work. The rest of you can catch up on your paperwork for now."

Everyone started to leave.

"Except you and Loblolly, Grave. I want to see both of you in my office—*now!*"

41

Captain Morgan rocked back and forth in his squeaky, high-backed executive chair, one of his favorite perks of office, staring silently at Grave and Loblolly, who sat opposite him, staring back. And then he stopped, the chair issuing a final shrill squeak. "I'm not opposed to office romances—"

Loblolly snapped at him. "There is no romance."

Morgan held up a hand and barked back. "Quiet!"

"She's right," said Grave.

"I said *quiet!*" Morgan wagged his finger at both of them. "Now, not another word until I'm finished saying what I'm saying."

Grave started to speak, but Morgan held up his hand, silencing him. "Not a word. Not a single word. Now, as I was saying, I am not opposed to office romances, but keep it out of the office. That display in the conference room was unnecessary and unprofessional, and I won't have it on my watch. Do you understand?"

Both nodded.

"You're both fine officers, fine detectives, and I expect the best from you on this case. Grave, I know of your past relationship with Ms. LaFarge, so I understand it may be difficult for you to think of her as a suspect. But, by god, she is, and you know it." He turned to Loblolly. "And you, I know jealousy when I see it, and I see it big time in you. Ms. LaFarge may be a suspect, but nothing so far has shown conclusively that she is anything else."

He began rocking in his chair again. "So here's the deal. One, take this romance or whatever you want to call it out of the office." He stopped rocking and pointed at Grave. "And there's a "B" for you, Grave. Going forward, I want you to focus on the employees at the winery. Charlize and Smithers-Watson will handle the family and their lawyer."

Morgan looked back and forth at them. "Have I made myself clear?"

"Yes, sir," said Loblolly.

Grave thought to object, but he knew that was useless with Morgan. Once that man made up his mind, it was made up, period. "Yes, captain."

Morgan put his palms on the desk and lifted himself to his feet with a grunt. "Now, get out there and catch the killers."

42

Detective Morgan Freeman sat in front of the Scanimation 465XL console, moving the slides and pushing the various knobs and buttons with an ease that had Detective Simon Grave whistling through his teeth.

"You've done this before," said Grave.

Freeman chuckled. "Many times, sir. It was my job before I joined the force as a patrolman."

"Why did you join the force when you're obviously so good at this scanimation business?"

"Being good at something doesn't mean it's what you should do in life. Perhaps it's just a short-circuit in my wiring, but I find scanimation a bit boring. It was wonderful at first, but once I learned all the tricks, it became too routine. The force offered me adventure."

Grave laughed. "Adventure? You call what we do adventure?"

"Yes, sir. Every day is different, at least now that I'm a detective, and I have you to thank for that, sir."

"No, I just recognized the talent in front of me. You were destined for this—or wired for it. In any case, you're a fine detective, so again, please drop the 'sir.' It's Grave when we're working and Simon when we're alone."

"Freeman. Morgan."

"Okay, Morgan, let's see your stuff."

"Right," said Morgan, turning back to the console. "I think we're about ready. I've uploaded the scans of the employees, the family, the lawyer, and that Save the Grapes guy, as well as the victim. Now, by pushing this button, the computer will create every possible scenario of killer-victim-killer."

"What do you mean killer-victim-killer?"

"Your Ms. Notion says she saw a tall figure grab the victim from behind and then a smaller figure delivered the death thrusts with the knife."

"Yes, exactly."

"Okay, let's take our Save the Grapes guy."

"Harry Smite."

"Yes. The computer will put him behind the victim and then match him with every other possible suspect. Then the computer will put him in front of the victim, wielding the knife. Then the computer will do the same for every other suspect. In the end we'll have every possible combination and permutation of possibilities. Assuming that is, we actually have the real killers in the data set and that Notion can make the match."

"It sounds both wonderfully scientific on one side and outrageously woo-woo on the other."

"You mean with Ms. Notion?"

"Precisely. Science versus a vision. And let me tell you, sometimes her visions are a notch or two off the mark. This whole exercise may be a bust."

Morgan nodded. "I guess we'll just have to see."

"Indeed," said Grave. "So, how long will this process take?"

"Processing will take a couple of hours."

"That long?" said Grave. "Look, I have something to do across town. Give me a buzz when you're finished."

"Okay, and I'll wait till you get back to show the images to Ms. Notion."

Grave thought a second and then shook his head. "No, no, let me know when you're ready, but proceed with Ida as soon as she shows up."

"Yes, sir."

"Simon."

"Um, right, Simon."

43

Charlize was giving Smithers-Watson a look that suggested she was not keeping up with his explanation of SyncVision.

"It's relatively simple, Charlize," he said. "We have a timeframe for the murder, correct?"

"Yes, a half-hour window."

"And we have scans of all the employees and family members."

"Indeed, we do."

So what SyncVision does is take all the footage from the many interior and exterior CCTV cameras, and sync them by time."

"Okay."

"But that's just step one. Step two is the heart of the matter. SyncVision takes our employee and family-member scans and determines every instance of their appearance on a camera within the system at the winery."

"Okay, and then what?"

"And then, using SyncVision, we can follow each and every employee and family member through our time window. Where they were at each second of that window, as well as trend lines showing in which direction and how fast they're moving."

"Brilliant, but what about visitors, people we haven't scanned?"

"Good question. When SyncVision comes upon the image of a person that does not match any of our employees or family members, it creates an Unknown Person identity and tracks that unknown person just like the people who've been scanned."

"So how do we proceed?"

"The analysis will take about ten minutes, and we're already seven minutes into that, so in about three minutes I'll be able to pull up a display showing the entire facility, inside and out, and a lot of dots showing everyone's location."

"Dots? I thought we'd see images of people."

"We start with dots, but we can then zoom in to see who that dot represents. But the dots can be very helpful, too. If we speed up the scenario, we can see trends. You know, if someone is running fast toward the crime scene or away from it, that movement might be key in finding our murderer or murderers."

"Nice."

"We can also just show the area where the crime takes place, and watch as dots appear and disappear during the crime window."

"Great, but that camera was down, right?"

"Yes, but we'll still be able to see when people disappeared into that blank zone, and when they came back out."

"Okay."

"And . . . and we can even lock on a single person and follow them through the timeframe and beyond. So, if we think Employee A was the culprit, we can follow their every action."

"And I assume we can then create a tape focusing solely on the murderer, for use in court."

Smithers-Watson nodded. "Indeed." He turned at the sound of a bell coming from the console. "Ah, here we are. Ready to roll."

Charlize smiled. "Okay, let's do this."

44

Grave had to get out of the station. He needed time to think and cool down from the dressing down by Morgan and the icy stares from Polly. A drive in the Sprite along the Third Intercoastal Highway would be just the thing to clear his head. The radio set at full volume, playing gospel music, would be high-decibel healing.

Once on the highway, though, he had a better idea and took the turn to the Crab Cove Cinema Cemetery for a visit with his friend Victoria, a young girl who had died in the eighteenth century and now served as a welcoming presence to the recently deceased.

Grave parked the Sprite in a spot closest to the path that led up to the bench where Victoria was usually waiting. He climbed out and waited for Barry to arrive.

"You're a little slow today," said Grave as Barry flew up and hovered in front of him.

"I had a word with Detective Loblolly's new drone, Sparky."

Grave looked concerned. "Oh, about what?"

"Not about Polly, of course. I would never do that without your permission. No, I was asking about any new features she might have. I was built several years ago, so I can't do many of the things she can do."

"Oh, like what?"

"Like split apart into as many as ten autonomous drones, each fully capable and each able to either work together with the others or work separately, totally independent."

"Wow."

"Indeed, sir." He waggled in the air. "Any chance of getting me such an upgrade?"

Grave frowned. "I can get you useful upgrades, but not the ability to split apart. That would require me to get a new drone to replace you."

Barry waggled in a negative way, or as negatively as he could manage. Most of his waggles looked exactly alike. "Oh, no, sir, I don't want you to do that."

"I didn't think so." Grave looked up the path. He could see Victoria waving at him. "Look, I'm going to visit with Victoria for a while. Why don't you check out the rest of the cemetery? They're always adding new features."

"Indeed, they are, sir. Enjoy your talk with your invisible friend, and I'll just have a look-see."

Barry buzzed off down a path that led to the grave of the Reverend Bendigo Bottoms. If Grave had time, he'd visit him as well. He usually had good advice, particularly as it related to life and love.

But now his major interest was speaking with Victoria. Maybe she had news about the arrival of Falcon Fontaine. He waved at her and began walking toward the bench.

45

Smithers-Watson tapped two buttons, and a two-dimensional representation of the interior and exterior of the winery popped up on the screen.

"Wait," said Charlize. "I thought we were going to see actual footage, not lines and blinking dots of light."

"Don't worry," said Smithers-Watson. "This is step one. The programmers who came up with SyncVision found that it is best to start with this representation. Users often found it difficult to follow the actual footage because of the many distractions in the background—trees, equipment, cars, and so on. When we see the patterns in the movement of the people, we'll be able to pull up the actual footage."

Charlize nodded. "Okay, so explain the lights to me."

"Each light identifies one specific person or simdroid. If it's blue, it's a day-shift employee. If it's green, it's a night-shift employee. Family members, their lawyer, and any of their staff are shown in yellow. And unknown people—visitors and so on—are shown in red. The victim, Mr. Fontaine, is represented by the purple light in this black arc, the area that would have been visible if that camera was working."

"So where do we start?"

"The simulation is set to begin at 6:30, the beginning of the timeframe for the murder, and end at 7:00, the end of the timeframe."

"So let's begin."

"One thing first. Although we currently are showing the half-hour timeframe, we have the data covering both shifts, both before and after the murder."

"So we can identify when people arrived and left."

"Exactly."

"All right, I'm good. Let's take a look."

Smithers-Watson tapped a button on the console and the dots of light began to move. "No, wait," he said, tapping the button again, stopping the simulation. "I've got it set on real time, so the simulation will take about half an hour to run. What we're looking for is movement into and out of the black arc surrounding the victim. The speed of the simulation doesn't matter, so I can speed this up to thirty seconds. Whether we go slow or fast, what we'll end up with at the end is a display showing who went into and out of that black arc. Once we have that, we can zero in on the movements of those people before, during, and after the murder."

"Well, let's go fast then."

"Fine," said Smithers-Watson. He adjusted a slide on the console and then hit the start button. The lights danced and swirled, each dot of light moving inside, outside, and throughout the facility and its surrounds.

"Wow," said Charlize. "It's like art with light."

Smithers-Watson chuckled. "It is."

They watched the black arc of the camera-free area with great interest, watching various lights moving into and out of it. And then the simulation stopped. All the lights disappeared except for those that had entered the black arc during the half-hour timeframe.

Three blue.

Two red.

Three yellow.

"There," said Smithers-Watson. "Now let's pull up each of those dots and find out who they are." He punched a series of buttons and a name appeared opposite each of the dots.

Charlize gasped. "Wow, I wasn't expecting that."

46

Victoria patted the bench, motioning Grave to sit next to her. "Come, Simon, sit down. You look worried. What's up?"

Grave was worried—about *everything* it seemed—but seeing Victoria, the little ghost in the yellow gingham dress, a red-headed girl with freckles, forever ten years old, always made him smile. He sat down next to her. "Oh, the usual. A new, troublesome case with multiple suspects."

"I think I know who you're talking about. Kind of short, speaks with a French accent, and a real pain in the you-know-what."

"Sounds like the man, all right. Falcon Fontaine, recently murdered."

Victoria nodded. "I thought he might be of interest to you, so I've already questioned him."

Grave sat up straight. "Really? What did he have to say?"

Victoria shrugged. "Unfortunately, not much. He's one of those dead folk who still thinks he's alive. He refuses to accept that he was stabbed repeatedly, even when the gaping wounds are pointed out to him. It's a terrible thing, denial. And not very productive."

Grave slumped back against the back of the bench. "Did you ask him what his last memory was? Who he was with?"

"Yes, but I'm afraid he didn't like the idea of last memory, and when I asked who was the last person he was with, he just shrugged and said, 'I'm a busy man. I was with everyone.'"

Grave sighed. "I assume he's in orientation now?"

Victoria rolled her eyes. "Well, he should be, but if you don't think you're dead, the last thing you want to do is attend an all-day seminar for the deceased."

"Do you think he'd talk to me?"

Victoria snorted. "Oh, no, not today, anyway. Let me work on him for a day or two. Most people eventually come around."

"I'd appreciate it, Victoria." He looked around the manicured grounds, every blade of grass seemingly designed to fill its little space. "So, how are you?"

She smiled. "You know, same old same old. Deal with the dead. Try to make them feel comfortable. Move them on when they're ready. Repeat, repeat, repeat."

Grave cocked his head. "What's that sound?"

Victoria threw up her hands. "The annoying rumble of heavy equipment. They're putting in a new section, for pets who pre-decease their owners. The idea is for their owners to join them at a later date, so they can be together again."

"Humph," said Grave. "Sounds like a good idea to me. I've never understood why owners and their pets should be in different graveyards."

"Indeed," said Victoria. "You should check it out on your way out. There are already a few dogs and cats interred there. And a pet duck, too."

Grave nodded. "I just might. Which direction is it?"

Victoria giggled. "Just follow the sound, Simon. Oh, and there's one grave you won't want to miss."

"Oh?"

"Yes, a dog named Shadow. They have a video of him snatching birds out of the air and racing around his yard. I couldn't believe it. He ran with the grace and power of a stallion. You simply must see it."

Grave smiled at her. "I will, I will, but first I have to have a little talk with the Reverend Bendigo Bottoms."

Victoria cocked her head and frowned. "Love troubles again?"

Grave sighed.

47

Ida Notion blinked her eyes repeatedly as Detective Morgan Freeman attempted to explain combinations and permutations to her. She had never been particularly fond of math, and now she was sure math was not particularly fond of her.

Freeman could see the confusion in her eyes. "Let me put it this way. We have thirty-seven people who want the last two seats to a ballgame. Turns out, that's 666 combinations."

Ida sighed. "I'm not sure how you got that number, but okay."

"Now, that's 666 combinations without regard to who is seated in Seat 6A and who is seated in seat 7A. Putting people in a specific seat brings us to permutations, and that number comes out to twice 666, or 1332."

"Um, I think I follow that, but will I really have to look at that many, um, whatchamacallits?"

"Scanimations. And the answer is no. There's another wrinkle here, and that involves the height of each person. You said one person in your vision was taller than the victim, and the other was shorter. Is that right?"

Ida closed her eyes and tried to bring the vision back. "Yes, that's right."

"Okay, so that brings the number of combinations and permutations down."

"To what? Sounds like I'm going to be here all day."

Freeman chuckled. "Let's not worry about the numbers. I have a way of reducing them."

"Oh?"

"Yes," he said. "Let me show you." He turned to the console and brought up a dozen black silhouettes showing a large figure holding on to a victim figure and a short figure confronting the victim figure. "Which of these most looks like your vision?"

Freeman watched Ida's eyes as she scanned the images from left to right and back again. Finally, she raised a finger and pointed at one image. "That one. Number seven."

"Good," said Freeman. He moved a cursor to that image and double-clicked on it. "Okay, I've isolated that combination. Now, let's animate it to make sure we've got the right one."

Ida smiled. "Okay."

Freeman pressed a key on the console and the figures began to move. "Is that what you saw in your vision?"

Ida cocked her head. "Mostly. But you have one thing wrong."

48

The Reverend Bendigo Bottoms shook his head, started to speak, then reconsidered, then shook his head, then finally spoke. "You're really telling me you're back to talking with a British accent?"

Grave started to speak, then reconsidered, worried that any words he had to say would come out as British as tea, then reconsidered again, then started to speak, and then stopped.

The reverend rolled his eyes. "Out with it, Simon."

Grave nodded and huffed out a sigh as long as a cricket stick. "Okay."

The reverend chuckled. "You see, that wasn't British at all, though I did detect a hint of a French accent."

Grave threw up his hands. "It's her."

"Lola?"

"Yes, every time I see her, the accent comes back."

The reverend put his hand on Grave's shoulder. "What we have here is a lack of confidence. Subconsciously you think the British accent lends a certain authority, a certain gravitas to whatever you're saying."

"Exactly what my therapist used to say."

"And how did he tell you to overcome it?"

"Didn't. Just told me to be aware of it and fight it off."

The reverend offered up his best sardonic chuckle. "Oh, that's rich. And nonproductive." He rubbed his hand on Grave's back. "Listen up, Simon, I think I know how to handle this."

Grave brightened. "Really?"

"Listen, I was a reverend for many, many years, and one of the important things I learned was how to get people to listen to me when all they wanted to do was sit in the pews, maybe sing a hymn or two, and go home, putting another checkmark on their church attendance sheet as if it was a way to punch their ticket to Heaven."

"And what did you learn, exactly."

The reverend raised a finger into the air and began moving it this way and that, gesticulating forcefully. "I learned this and this and this."

"Gestures, you mean?"

"Exactly. Believe me, there is more power in a thrust or pointed finger than in a British accent."

"So you want me to use my finger?"

"Yes, yes. Think about it, Simon. When you think to open your mouth, think about your finger and how it can help you."

"Um."

"First, think of it as a signal, a memory device. Before you open your mouth, just think of your finger. That should prevent you from using the British accent."

"Okay."

"Then use that finger. Raise it, point it, swirl it in the air, jab it at a person, let it sweep the room as you speak. Everyone who sees you doing this will yield to your authority."

Grave nodded slowly. "You think?"

The reverend laughed. "Oh, son, I know, I know." The reverend suddenly had another thought. "Say, did you ever read *Bleak House*?"

"You mean Dickens?"

"Yes."

"No."

The reverend waved a hand in front of his face. "Doesn't matter. Anyway, there's a character in that book called Inspector Bucket. He's a detective, just like you, and he uses his finger to control every situation. Waves it about. Waggles it. Points it. Why, he is a veritable master of the finger."

"I'll have to read it."

"No, no, you miss my point. Just use that finger of yours to take command."

Grave smiled at him. "All right, I'll give it a shot."

"That's the ticket," said the reverend, giving a firm slap to Grave's shoulder. Or at least he tried to. His hand actually went right through Grave's shoulder.

Grave frowned and let out another long sigh. "But there's still the problem of Polly."

The reverend shook his head. "We've been through this before. Love is like a chocolate donut, remember?"

"I do, and I agree with how you explained that the last time we talked about Polly, but still—"

Grave was cut short by Barry, who zoomed up between Grave and the reverend. "Sir, Captain Morgan was just on the horn. We need to get to the station post haste. The results of the scanimation and the SyncVision are in. Everyone is assembling."

"Go, Simon," said the reverend. "We can pick this up another time."

"Right, right," said Grave. "Okay, Barry, let's go."

The reverend called after him. "Don't forget to give them the finger!"

49

Detective Morgan Freeman waited until everyone was around the conference table before bringing up the first screen shot from the scanimations. "Who killed Falcon Fontaine? Who held his arms? Who delivered the fatal stab wounds? The hope was that the scanimations you are about to see would clearly identify the killers." He paused and looked over at Captain Morgan. "Unfortunately, captain, there are no clear results." He watched as Captain Morgan rolled his eyes. "But we did reduce the field of possibilities."

"So who are the prime suspects?"

"I'll get to that, captain, but first let me tell you how I got to this point."

Morgan waved his hand. "Okay, go on."

"I met with Ms. Ida Notion, the psychic, for about three hours. In an effort to reduce the number of scanimations she would have to watch, I presented her with a range of silhouette images showing the murder in progress. She selected one of those images as a 'best fit' for her vision. I then proceeded to run that scanimation for her, which identified Jacob Dilby, the family attorney, and Angus McBride, the maintenance engineer, as the perpetrators."

Grave slapped a hand on the table. "So we've got our men. Wonderful!" He shot a glance at Polly. He just knew it couldn't be Lola.

Polly sneered back.

"Not so fast," said Freeman. "I said there were no clear results. Ida didn't recognize either one. Said her vision was pretty blurry. So, with that in mind, I plugged in the heights of Dilby and McBride, and looked for scanimations involving people plus or minus half an inch in height. And that involved additional possibilities."

"How many possibilities?" said Captain Morgan.

"Six suspects in all, including Blanche LaTour, the secretary, Harry Smite of Save the Grapes—"

Detective Snoot gasped.

"Something you want to say, Snoot?" said the captain.

She shook her head. "No, sir, sorry to interrupt." She looked over at Polly, whose mouth was open.

"Go on, then, Freeman. Who else?"

"Um, Smite, Art Travis Tee, and Lola LaFarge."

Now it was time for Polly to slap her hand on the table and for Grave's mouth to drop open.

"Let's bring them all in, then," said Morgan.

Freeman held up a hand. "Two things first, sir. Yes, we have six suspects, but if I change the parameters again just by a quarter of an inch either way, the number of suspects increases to twelve. And that brings me to the second point. Since my results are shaky at best, I suggest we hear from Charlize and Smithers-Watson before drawing any conclusions. I mean, my scanimations are based on a vision, not on hard facts."

"That sounds reasonable, Freeman. So, can I turn this over to Charlize and Smithers-Watson?"

Freeman started to say yes, but then stopped. "One more thing, a little detail Ms. Notion remembered about her vision."

"Go on."

"We had our scanimation killer stabbing upward into Fontaine's chest, but Notion was certain the stabs were coming down on his chest."

Morgan huffed. "Up, down, and blurry. What does it matter?"

Jeremy Polk, the medical examiner, cleared his throat as a way of taking the floor. "Her vision matches the wounds, captain. All the stabs were at a downward angle."

Captain Morgan shrugged. "I don't know how that will help us, but okay, the killer stabbed at a downward angle."

"One more thing," said Polk. "While I have the floor, I want to add a new piece to the puzzle. Results of the autopsy show that Mr. Fontaine was terminally ill with stage four colon cancer. My guess is he would have lived at most another two months."

"Wow," said Polly. "So the killers either didn't know or didn't care he was going to die anyway."

Grave could feel a British accent coming on, so he thrust a finger high into the air, perhaps too dramatically for the situation. "You can't hide cancer. The treatments. The loss of hair. His family would know. Most of his employees would know."

He stopped talking, then realized he had left his finger in the air, and then pulled it down. "At least that's what I think."

"Your point is well taken, Grave," said Polk, "but let me clarify. His cancer was *undiagnosed* or just recently diagnosed. There is no sign of any kind of treatment whatsoever."

Morgan drummed his fingers on the table, then turned to Charlize. "Six suspects, maybe more. Can you narrow the field for us, Charlize?"

Charlize gave everyone a quick smile. "Well, maybe, but it's, um, *complicated*."

"Oh, great," said Morgan, rubbing a hand over his face. "Well, go on, let's hear it."

50

Charlize stood and walked over to the full-wall monitor displaying a static image of the many colored lights of the SyncVision simulation. "What you see here is a display of all the people present within the field of view of the inoperable camera that covered — or in fact, didn't cover — the crime scene."

Morgan huffed. "We need more than colored lights, Charlize."

Charlize rolled her eyes. "I'm aware of that sir. Just setting the stage, so everyone understands the import of the colors."

"Very well," said Morgan. "What's with the colors?"

"Each light represents one person. The victim, Mr. Fontaine, is depicted by the purple light here in this black arc, what we can call the kill box. Day-shift employees are blue, night-shift green, family members yellow, including their lawyer and household staff."

"What about all those red lights?" said Morgan.

"Unknown people. Visitors. Tourists."

"So, if I'm hearing you correctly," said Morgan, "we have three day-shift employees, two strangers, and three from the family member slash staff slash lawyer grouping."

"Yes, exactly," said Charlize, then turned to Smithers-Watson. "Bring up the identities."

The dots were replaced with camera images.

"Wow," said Freeman.

"Yes, wow is right," said Charlize. "The people in the kill box included Lola LaFarge, her brother Frankie Fontaine, Blanche LaTour, Art Travis Tee, Angus McBride, Harry Smite, the lawyer Jacob Dilby, and an unknown man."

Freeman spoke up. "So all of my suspects plus Frankie Fontaine and that unknown man."

"Who is that guy?" said Morgan.

"I don't know," said Grave, "but we best find him."

Morgan drummed his fingers on the table. "In any event, the SyncVision results are very close to the scanimation results."

"So it seems," said Charlize, "but as I said, it's complicated."

"All right, I'll bite," said Morgan. "How is it complicated?"

Charlize turned to Polk. "Jeremy, how confident are you in your half-hour timeframe for the murder?"

Polk blinked. "Well, I'd say it's fairly accurate."

"Fairly?"

"Yes, plus or minus ten minutes either way."

Charlize turned back to Morgan. "Here's the complication, sir. If we move the timeframe back ten minutes, we'd have a different set of suspects, and if we move the timeframe forward, the same thing. And in that last instance—moving it forward ten minutes—Lola LaFarge and her brother drop from the list of suspects."

Morgan whistled through his teeth. It was not a happy whistle. Or a sad whistle. It was, in fact, a complicated whistle.

51

Captain Morgan sat quietly for a few moments, drumming his fingers on the table. "So, what I'm hearing is that we have suspects based on a vision, and suspects based on a timeframe that may or may not be accurate." He looked around the room. "Well, that's just great."

Charlize raised a hand. "It's a quandary, yes, but we may be able to break it down, find out who did what when."

"And how would we do that?" said Morgan.

"The tapes from the cameras are time-stamped, so we can lock down the movements of everyone in the facility."

Morgan brightened. "Of course."

"And I think the starting point is the time when Falcon Fontaine actually stepped into the kill box," said Charlize. She turned to Smithers-Watson. "Show us the movement of Falcon Fontaine."

Smithers-Watson pressed a button and keyed in Fontaine's name. The tape began rolling, showing Fontaine in his office, then moving out of the office and across the vineyard floor toward the fermentation tank. "And then he disappeared from view as he entered the kill box," said Smithers-Watson, "at precisely 6:22 p.m."

Grave thrust a finger into the air. "And who else was in the kill box at that time?"

Smithers-Watson pressed a series of buttons. Lights appeared of different colors, each moving into the kill box. Smithers-Watson pressed another button and the lights transformed into images of everyone in the kill box.

"Wow," said Grave, waving his finger in the air and then pointing it at the images on the screen. "That's a lot of people."

"Okay," said Charlize, "what we have here, it seems to me, is the last tour of the day by that simdroid Bacchus, who appears to be leading a group of eleven people. So we have Bacchus, the tourists, Fontaine, and Angus McBride, the maintenance engineer. Oh, and Harry Smite, who seems to have joined the tour group."

Morgan held up a hand. "I can see how this is going to get complicated, so before we continue, I'd like to let everyone know that Detective Grave and I have decided that because of his previous relationship with Ms. LaFarge, someone else should take the lead with her and the family. So, going forward, Charlize will be the lead on the family. Snoot and Loblolly will focus on the employees, and Grave will take Smite, the lawyer, and that as yet unidentified person." He looked around the room to see if there were any objections. Smithers-Watson had his hand raised.

"Yes, Smithers?"

"I assume I'm with Charlize, right?"

Morgan shook his head. "No, actually, I want you to stay here and squeeze every nuance out of the SyncVision."

"And me sir?" said Detective Freeman. "With Grave, I assume."

"Yes, with Grave." He looked around the room. "So, everyone okay with their roles?" He didn't wait for replies, but turned back to Charlize. "Okay, back to you, Charlize."

52

Charlize and Smithers-Watson walked the team through the SyncVision scenarios, person by person, minute by minute.

At 6:22 p.m., Falcon Fontaine entered the kill box, joining an eleven-visitor tour led by Bacchus. Angus McBride, the maintenance engineer, was also there, along with Harry Smite of Save the Grapes.

By 6:23 p.m., the tour had left the kill box, but Smite and McBride remained, along with Fontaine. Art Travis Tee, the assistant vintner, joined this group just seconds into the minute.

At 6:24 p.m., nothing had changed.

But at 6:25 p.m., Smite and Tee left, each moving quickly. Cameras showed Smite running across the parking lot. Tee appeared to be speed-walking down a hallway to his office laboratory. Likewise, cameras showed LaFarge and her brother, Frankie, racing into the building and heading directly up to and into the kill zone.

At 6:26 p.m., McBride left.

At 6:31 p.m., one minute into the original half-hour timeframe, Lafarge and Frankie Fontaine leave the kill box, moving quickly to a limousine that quickly flew away.

At 6:33 p.m., McBride returned, along with Tee and LaTour.

At 6:34 p.m., Tee and LaTour left, each moving quickly.

At 6:40, McBride left, moving slowly.

At 6:45, Two limousines arrived in front of the building, one carrying Jacob Dilby, the family lawyer, and the other carrying the mystery man. The men seemed to know each other, and walked together to Fontaine's office.

At 6:48 p.m., Dilby, LaTour, and the mystery man entered the kill zone.

At 6:50p.m., the mystery man could be seen exiting the kill zone and moving quickly to his limousine, which promptly drove away. A close-up but blurry image of the man's face seemed to suggest he was angry.

At 6:52 p.m., LaTour and Dilby leave the kill zone and return to Fontaine's office.

At 7:00 p.m, Dilby leaves the office and the building, and drives away in his limousine.

At 7:03 p.m., LaTour turns out the lights in Fontaine's office and leaves the building.

At 7:04 p.m, in the kill zone, nothing happens.

At 7:10 p.m., nothing continues to happen.

53

Everyone started shouting at once, each shouting out the name or names they felt certain were the murderers.

Captain Morgan slammed a hand down on the table, silencing everyone. "Let's not get ahead of ourselves, people. I have my ideas about this, too, but let's be thorough and methodical." He turned to Charlize. "So, the thought provided us by Ms. Notion's vision was that two people killed Fontaine. What pairs did we discover in this analysis of yours?"

Charlize nodded back at Morgan. "If you study the scenario, there are two time periods where two people are alone with Fontaine. The first is a McBride-Smite pairing, followed by a Dilby-LaTour pairing." She paused and looked around the room. "But what if Ms. Notion was wrong about her vision or only saw part of what happened? In that case we have no fewer than four scenarios involving three people and one scenario involving one person."

"What are those?" said Morgan.

"Okay, in order, we have Smite-McBride-Tee, followed by LaFarge-Frankie-McBride, followed by McBride-Tee-LaTour, followed by Dilby, LaTour, and the mystery man."

"And the single-person scenario is McBride, right?" said Morgan.

"Yes," said Charlize. "And in fact, McBride appears in five of the seven possibilities."

Grave raised a finger into the air and waggled it back and forth. "Obviously, we need to re-interview each of these people, particularly McBride. But there is still a basic question we need to consider going forward." Grave paused to look at Captain Morgan.

"Go on, Grave."

"First, even now, are we sure we have the right timeframe? Is 6:22 to 7:10 it? Or did the murder take place later?"

Smithers-Watson raised a hand. "It's possible, but unlikely. The next person to enter the kill box was a maintenance technician, at 9:50 p.m., who stayed in the box for just fifteen seconds. Certainly not enough time to murder someone and dispose of the body. After that, we have several people passing through and not stopping. So no, Grave, a different timeframe is a remote possibility at best."

"So I was only off eight to ten minutes or so," said Polk. "I'd say that's pretty good."

"What else, Grave?" said Morgan.

"That's all, sir. For now."

"Okay, then," said Morgan, turning back to the group. "You have your assignments and you know the scenarios that took place within the timeframe. Get out there and talk to the suspects. Check out their stories, and let's see if we can nail this case down—quickly."

Everyone pushed back their chairs and began leaving, but Morgan wasn't quite finished. "And you, Grave. Find that mystery man."

Grave nodded. "Yes, sir."

"And Grave?"

"Yes, sir."

"Please stop with the British accent and all that finger waving. It's really annoying."

Grave started to speak and wave a finger in his defense, but just nodded and rushed from the room.

54

Detectives Snoot and Loblolly found Angus McBride in the break room of Château de Crabe Rouge, looking none too happy to see them.

"Let me guess," he said. "Cops."

Snoot nodded. "Detectives, actually. Mind if we sit down?"

McBride rolled his eyes. "Free country." He waved his hand at the two chairs opposite him. "Have a seat."

Snoot and Loblolly sat down, McBride taking the opportunity to look them up and down. "Why are such attractive women such as yourselves working for the police?"

Snoot sneered at him. "Please."

He shrugged. "I'm just saying."

Loblolly looked him in the eye. "Well don't. Now, we have some additional questions for you."

"I already told those simdroid detectives everything I know. I last saw Fontaine when he rushed by me, looking all angry like, down by the fermentation tanks. And that's it."

Snoot nodded, then shook her head. "Well, the thing is, that's only part true. You left a few things out."

McBride tried to brush off the remark, but he seemed to be shaken, at least a little. "I saw him. He rushed by me. That's it."

Loblolly shook her head. "You see, that's really not what happened, is it?"

"It is, I swear."

"No," said Snoot. "You've left a lot out. The CCTV cameras show you moving into the area of the fermentation tanks at 6:20 p.m. Two minutes later, Fontaine enters the same area, an area you don't leave until 6:26."

"That can't be right."

"Oh, but it is," said Loblolly. "So, was there anyone else with you during those four minutes?"

His eyes darted back and forth between them, looking for a safe place to land, but found only hard stares. "No, like I said, we just passed each other."

Snoot raised her voice. "For four minutes?"

Loblolly jumped back in. "Answer my question. Who else was there?"

"Just me and Fontaine."

"So you had four minutes to kill him and put him in the fermentation tank?"

McBride jumped to his feet. "No, like I said, I would never kill the man."

"Sit back down," said Snoot. She pointed at his chair. "Sit!"

McBride reluctantly sat. "You've got this all wrong."

"Have we?" said Loblolly. "Turns out there was a tour group, Bacchus, Tee, and a guy named Harry Smite. And you were then joined by Fontaine's son and daughter."

He shook his head. "I don't remember. Maybe, I guess. And what of it? I mean, how could I kill the man with so many others around? And I'm not saying there were. And who the hell is Harry Smite?"

Snoot smiled at him. "Let's move on, shall we?"

McBride rolled his eyes. "Move on to what?"

"To 6:33," said Loblolly. "That's when you come back to the area."

"Come back?" He looked at the ceiling, trying to remember. "If you say so. I mean, I'm the maintenance engineer. I'm here, there, and everywhere all day."

Loblolly ignored his response. "You come back, and you're there with Tee and LaTour and Fontaine."

He looked down at the table and continued shaking his head. "No, no, no."

"And then they leave and you're alone with Fontaine again for a full *six* minutes."

"No."

Snoot jumped in. "Six minutes, McBride, and we know that's true."

"I did nothing!" he shouted. "Nothing!"

Snoot held up a hand. "Let's take a step back."

"Back? To what?"

"To the beginning. Your call to Fontaine, summoning him to inspect the tank."

"Call? I made no call."

Snoot and Loblolly glanced at one another.

"Seriously," said McBride, "the next tank to be inspected was number six and that wasn't supposed to happen until the following morning."

"So," said Loblolly, "you must have been surprised to see him come storming up to you at the fermentation tank."

"A little, maybe, but like I said, he just stormed past me."

Snoot shook her head. "And, what, *disappeared?* We have him in that area from 6:22 on, and you were in the same place—the same *damned* place—for over ten minutes. Together. With him."

McBride took a deep breath. "That's just not true."

"Then what?"

McBride shrugged. "I don't know. Maybe he went out the back door?"

Snoot's eyes went wide. "The back door?"

McBride nodded. "Yes, the emergency exit behind the fermentation tank."

Loblolly's mouth dropped open a bit more than Snoot's.

55

Jacob Dilby, attorney at law, seemed annoyed that Grave and Freeman had shown up at his office. "So what is it now?" he said. "I thought we'd pretty much covered everything."

Grave shrugged. "I said I'd follow up."

Dilby looked at his watch. "I have a client in two minutes, so can we speed this up. How can I help you?"

Grave smiled at him. "Well, perhaps you can explain why you lied about your whereabouts on the evening of the murder."

"Lied? I didn't lie. I was right here at 7:15. My secretary can confirm that. Or you can check the CCTV cameras around the square."

Grave leaned forward in his chair, the movement prompting a squeak from the leather. "But from 6:45 p.m. to 7:00 p.m. you were at the Château de Crabe Rouge, with Fontaine, LaTour, and an unknown man."

Dilby leaned forward in his chair, which also offered a squeak of leather. "With LaTour, yes, and one of my clients, Sebastian Smythe, owner of the Château du Nez Bleu. I was coordinating a deal between him and Fontaine, but Fontaine was a no-show."

Detective Freeman found the squeak in his own leather chair, rocking forward to ask, "What kind of deal?"

Dilby slumped back in his chair, adding another squeak. "I don't think I can get into that. It's all confidential."

Grave moved forward in his chair as slowly as he dared, trying to prevent a squeak, but failed. "Your client is dead, and the deal could be of importance to our investigation." He rocked back, causing another squeak. "And you know full well we can get the information through other means."

Dilby looked at his watch, and sighed. "All right. Fontaine was attempting to sell a forty-percent share in his vineyard."

Grave's eyes widened. "Sell? I thought they were fierce competitors."

"They are, or were, but Fontaine needed cash."

"Cash for what?" said Freeman.

Dilby rolled his eyes. "For a ridiculous venture."

Grave squeaked forward again. "And that would be . . .?"

"The first vineyard on Mars."

"Mars?" said Freeman.

"Mars?" said Grave.

Dilby nodded at them. It was a squeakless moment. "Yes, other vineyards had failed at creating wine on Mars, but the thing is, they all tried growing hydroponic grapes, and failed. Mr. Fontaine's wine, by contrast, only involves chemicals, alcohol, and nanobots, all things that can be made on Mars."

"I see," said Grave. "But it still seems odd that he'd give his competitor a large share of his company in exchange for cash."

Dilby nodded. "I know, but the thing is, it was Fontaine's dream. And sometimes, when you let your dream take over, you make mistakes."

Freeman squeaked forward again. "But the deal didn't go through. Fontaine was murdered first."

"So it seems," said Dilby.

"Which benefits anyone in line for inheritance," said Grave.

Dilby raised his eyebrows. "Yes, of course."

"Speaking of which," said Grave, "um, when will the will be read?"

Dilby smiled. "I was about to tell you. It'll be tomorrow morning at nine, at the vineyard. So many people are named that we've decided to hold the reading at the workplace."

"Well," said Grave. "We'll certainly be there."

Dilby blinked. "Be there? Why on earth—"

Grave squeaked forward again. "To see who gains by the death of Fontaine and this quashed deal with Smythe."

"Very well," said Dilby. "I'll make sure there will be extra chairs for you and Detective Freeman."

"Good," said Grave. "Now, back to my questions."

Dilby rolled his eyes, and squeaked. "I thought we were through here."

"Not quite. So, at precisely 6:52 p.m. you and Ms. LaTour returned to Fontaine's office, where you stayed for eight minutes."

Dilby threw up his hands. "I honestly don't know where you're going with this. Fontaine didn't show up, Smythe stormed out of the building, and Blanche and I went back to the office, hoping Fontaine would show up."

"And what did you talk about?" said Freeman.

"Talk? We didn't talk. She had work to do, so I just sat there a few minutes. Then Fontaine continued to be a no-show, so I left and came back here." He looked back and forth at Freeman and Grave. "So, is that it?"

Grave looked at Freeman, who shrugged.

"Yes," said Grave. "That's it—for now."

Grave and Freeman stood, their chairs offering a symphony of squeaks as the leather sought to return to its unburdened form.

56

Charlize sat opposite Lola LaFarge and her brother, Frankie, staring intently at them but not saying anything, or at least not yet. She had found in the past that a preliminary discomfiting moment for a suspect often led to a quicker resolution of the crime at hand.

Lola LaFarge stared back at her with a mix of defiance and wariness. Frankie, on the other hand, stared back with a mix of boredom and dismissiveness. He didn't seem the least bit concerned.

Finally, Charlize broke the silence. "Your previous comments about your whereabouts on the evening of the murder, namely that you were here in this very library, seem to fly in the face of the facts."

LaFarge started to speak, then paused, considering how best to begin. "Detective, our whereabouts at 7:00 p.m. on that evening was here, as corroborated by our butler. Surely, Simon must have mentioned that."

Charlize smiled back at her. "Oh, indeed he did. However, the CCTV cameras at the vineyard clearly show you and your brother arriving there at 6:25 p.m. and leaving at 6:31 p.m., a time period well within the time-of-death timeframe and sufficient enough in length for you and your brother here to kill your father and make your escape."

Frankie leaned forward in his chair and sneered. "That is true, except for the part about us killing our father, which is pure nonsense. Yes, we were there—briefly—but yes again, we were here in the library by seven. We have a flying limo, you see."

Charlize nodded. "And why were you at the vineyard?"

Frankie slumped back in his chair. "To try and stop him from making a financial blunder."

"By killing him?" said Charlize.

Frankie rolled his eyes. "No, detective, by trying to talk some sense into him."

"And how did that talk go?"

"Not at all," said LaFarge. "He wasn't there."

Charlize cocked her head. "It's curious, though, don't you think, that you went directly to the scene of the crime and not to your father's office?"

LaFarge shrugged. "We called ahead. Blanche, father's secretary, told us where he was, or rather, where he should be."

"But when you got there and he wasn't there, surely you would have tried to find him. Go to his office, for example."

"Of course," said LaFarge. "We called Blanche again, but she didn't know where he was. We thought perhaps that he was already on his way home."

"So we came back home as fast as we could," said Frankie.

"To this library?"

Both nodded.

"Where you had an argument at precisely 7:00 p.m."

LaFarge and Frankie looked at each other, and then LaFarge spoke. "A disagreement on how best to proceed, and who should take the lead in approaching father."

Charlize leaned forward. "This financial transaction. What was it to be?"

LaFarge sighed and looked at Frankie, who rolled his eyes.

"He was going to sell a forty-percent share in our vineyard to our major competitor," he said. "The Château du Nez Bleu."

Charlize blinked. "The blue nose?"

"Yes," said LaFarge. "He had this silly dream of building the first vineyard on Mars. It consumed him."

"And why do you think it was silly?"

LaFarge shook her head. "The Mars Colony isn't big enough to support a vineyard. The numbers just didn't work. Not only would we be giving away forty percent of our company, we'd be throwing all our remaining money at a worthless, foolhardy venture. It would have ruined us."

Charlize sat back in her chair. "But with your father out of the way, the deal couldn't go through and your inheritance would remain safe."

LaFarge and Frankie glanced at one another, then looked away, not wanting to meet each other's eyes or Charlize's. Both seemed to retreat to their previous states: LaFarge defiant and wary, Frankie bored and dismissive.

Charlize just stared at them for some seconds, and then said, "One more question, if you don't mind."

57

Captain Morgan's drone, Rum, came roaring into the conference room, swinging his little cutlass with as much swash and buckle as he could manage. "Captain, we have just received an urgent message-slash-request from Detectives Snoot and Loblolly."

Captain Morgan, who had been looking over the shoulder of Smithers-Watson, reviewing the SyncVision tapes, turned and barked at Rum. "Okay, man, what is it?"

Rum hovered to a stop in front of Morgan's nose. "Sir, Detectives Snoot and Loblolly report that there is an emergency exit in the area covered by the inoperable camera."

"What?" shouted Morgan, anger growing in him, his face approaching beet red with preternatural speed. "How could we have missed this? Get me Polk on the line. No, you get him on the line and tell him to get his medical backside out there with a forensics team."

"Yes, sir, but there's more. Snoot said she and Loblolly would secure the area and check it out, but they'd like Smithers-Watson here to see if there's anything on the SyncVision that might show someone coming into or out of the crime scene through that door."

Morgan turned to Smithers-Watson. "Did you hear that?"

Smithers-Watson was already throwing switches, dialing dials, and punching buttons, the images on the screen switching back and forth between the cameras on the outside of the building. "It will take a couple of minutes, sir, but let me show you something else while we're waiting."

Morgan perked up. "Something else?"

"Yes, take a look here, on the secondary monitor."

Morgan leaned over Smithers-Watson's shoulder. "What the—"

58

Grave and Freeman walked out into the bright sunlight of the town square. "What did you think?" said Grave.

"I don't trust him."

"Neither do I." Grave turned and looked down the block. Skunk 'n Donuts was just a few stores down, and he wondered whether they should take the time to have a chocolate donut. Then he remembered that Freeman was a simdroid. "So, let's head over to Harry Smite's so-called office. And then we'll finish up at that blue nose vineyard."

"Sounds like a plan," said Freeman. "But can I ask you a question first? I mean, before we climb into the Sprite."

"Sure," said Grave. "What is it?"

"I couldn't help noticing that you and Detective Loblolly are not getting along."

Grave puffed out his cheeks. "I guess you could say that."

"It's that LaFarge woman, isn't it?"

"I guess. I wasn't ever expecting to have her back in my life."

"You had a relationship?"

"For a few months. She was the governess at the Hawthorne Mansion in a case I worked a few years ago."

"What happened?"

"We were just, I don't know, not that compatible."

"Like what?"

"She had expensive tastes and liked nights out on the town."

"And you're pretty much a homebody."

"Yes."

"I could see that when you took me to your place. You just want to chill after a long day."

"Exactly."

"LaFarge seems like a strong woman. Are you afraid of strong women?"

"No, not at all. In fact, I prefer them."

"Well, I'd say Polly is a strong woman, wouldn't you?"

"Yes, but I think that's pretty much over."

"Because she saw your reaction to LaFarge. That there's something still unresolved about your relationship."

Grave sighed. "Yes, or at least I thought there was, or might be."

"And that's why you lapse into that British accent of yours?"

"Yes."

"And now the finger pointing and jabbing to replace the accent?"

"Yes, you noticed that?"

Freeman chuckled. "Everyone did. It looked like you were having some sort of fit."

Grave rolled his eyes. "I was told it would work."

Freeman shook his head. "No, not at all. Listen, you are Detective Simon Grave, the *famous* Detective Simon Grave. You don't need crutches. Be yourself, man. Be yourself."

Grave gave Freeman a look. "What, are you a therapist now? Did Freeman ever play that role?"

Freeman shrugged. "I don't know. All I know is that it would be a damned shame if you and Polly didn't get together."

"Doubtful now. I think she's written me off."

"I hope not."

"Anyway," said Grave, walking toward the Sprite, "we'd better get moving."

Freeman started to follow, but Grave suddenly stopped. "Wait, I just thought of something."

"What?"

"About the case."

"What?"

Grave wheeled in place. "Where's that drone of mine."

Freeman looked down the street. "There, by the Skunk 'n Donuts."

Grave spotted him and began running toward him. "Wait here. I'll be right back."

Freeman watched as Grave rushed up to Barry and began speaking. Barry waggled at whatever Grave had said, and sped away, gaining altitude quickly before disappearing entirely.

Grave raced back down the street to Freeman. "Come on, let's go."

"What was that all about?"

"Just a hunch. I'll tell you later."

Grave motioned him into the Sprite and they were soon speeding across town, the leaves on the trees shaking as the high-decibel Sprite sped by.

59

Snoot and Loblolly made sure the crime scene around the emergency door was secure and that Officer Larrys were positioned around it before making their way to the office of Blanche LaTour.

LaTour welcomed them with a grimace and motioned them reluctantly into two office chairs designed to discourage long visits. "What can I do for you *now*," she said, the "now" freighted with her belief that *everything* had been done for them and that this "now" was nothing less than an unnecessary intrusion on her day.

Snoot fought the grimace with a smile that seemed to say, *watch it, bitch, I'm in control now.* "Just a few follow-up questions. Won't take long."

"Good, I'm very busy." She slumped back into her chair and crossed her arms. "Okay, what?"

Loblolly cleared her throat. "We've been going over the CCTV footage and would like to clarify a few things with you."

"Go on."

"Mr. Fontaine arrived at the fermentation tank at precisely 6:22 p.m. Eleven minutes later, you, Mr. McBride, and Mr. Tee arrived at the tank. Why were you there?"

"I was looking for Mr. Fontaine. He was supposed to meet with the lawyer and another gentleman, and he was going to be late. I didn't want him to be late."

"Did you find Mr. Fontaine?" said Snoot.

"No, I did not. I asked McBride and Tee about his whereabouts, but neither had seen him."

"So what did you do?" said Loblolly.

"I went back to my office."

"Did you not think to call his drone?" said Snoot.

"Mr. Fontaine was not fond of drones in the workplace. He rarely used his and frowned on those who did."

"So," said Loblolly, "you're back in your office. What happened there?"

"I did my job, end-of-the-month stuff, and then, about fifteen minutes later, the lawyer and a Mr. Smythe showed up. I told them Mr. Fontaine had gone missing, but they insisted we look for him. So we went back to the area around the fermentation tank. Of course, he wasn't there."

"So they left," said Snoot.

LaTour nodded. "Mr. Smythe, yes, He was very angry."

"And Dilby?" said Loblolly.

"He went back with me to the office, waited a few minutes, hoping Fontaine would show up, but then left."

"Was he angry?" said Snoot.

"More annoyed, I'd say."

"So now you're alone in the office," said Snoot. "What did you do?"

"It was the end of my workday, so I straightened my desk, turned out the lights, and went home."

"Weren't you concerned about the whereabouts of Mr. Fontaine?" said Snoot.

LaTour sighed. "Mr. Fontaine did things without regard to me or, in fact, anyone. He'd disappeared at the end of the day before, so I assumed he'd just gone home. I mean, his limousine was parked out there, waiting for him."

"With the chauffer?" said Loblolly.

"No, the chauffer delivered the limo, but left. He was given the evening off, you see."

"And how do you know this?" said Snoot.

"He called me."

Snoot looked around. "I don't see any drones? How did you receive a call?"

LaTour rolled her eyes. "We have fixed drones at various locations in the facility. They don't fly. They're built in."

Snoot continued looking around.

LaTour looked up at the ceiling. "Felix, say hello to the detectives."

The voice was low and deep and seemed to be coming from every direction. "Hello," said the voice. "How may I be of help?"

60

Grave and Freeman found Harry Smite at his "office" next to the dumpster, sitting at his desk, making a protest sign that read "Real Grapes!" in a bold burgundy.

"Mr. Smite," said Grave, "I'm Detective Simon Grave and this is my partner, Detective Morgan Freeman. We'd like to ask you a few questions."

Smite looked up from his sign and nodded at them. "I already talked to the police. Two female detectives. I don't think I have anything more to offer."

"Well," said Grave, "perhaps that's true, but questions remain."

"Such as?"

"Although you told the, um, female detectives that you were outside the building, we actually have you on camera inside the building, at the same time and at the same location of the murder victim, Mr. Falcon Fontaine."

Smite's eyes went wide. "Me? On Camera? Are you sure?"

"Yes, definitely," said Freeman.

Smite put the sign aside and scratched his chin. "I suppose that's possible. Yes, yes, you know what, I think you're right. It was at the end of the day, right? The last tour?"

"Yes," said Grave. "We have you there for about two minutes, from 6:23 p.m. to 6:25 p.m."

"Yeah, yeah, I snuck in with the last tour group, for the final tasting of the day." He spread his arms to indicate his office. "As you can see, I live humbly. A chance for cheese and crackers is something I always take advantage of."

"Of course," said Grave. "And what did you see when you were with the tour group?"

"A lot of people I didn't know, a couple of employees, that huge simdroid named Bacchus—man, is he ever a wonder—and that bastard, Falcon Fontaine."

Freeman's eyes went wide. "You actually saw him?"

"Yes, or rather, he saw me, and was none too pleased. I thought he was going to kill me, he was so angry, so I beat it out of there pronto." He turned to Grave and chuckled. "I don't think I've ever run so fast."

"I see," said Grave. "And then, as you're running out, you see Lola LaFarge and her brother, Frankie Fontaine, arriving."

"That's right, and Fontaine must have been angry with them, too, because they came running back out four or five minutes later, and flew away in that amazing flying limo of theirs. Boy, would I like to take just one ride in that thing."

"I bet," said Grave. "Now, after that, did you see anything else?"

Smite shook his head. "Nope. I left. I was tired and hungry—never did get my cheese and crackers—so I left. You know, maybe a minute after that limo. I was too involved in packing up to notice anything else."

"All right," said Grave. "You've been very helpful."

Grave and Freeman turned to leave.

"So," said Smite. "Are you guys going to be at the reading of the will tomorrow?"

Grave turned back. "What?"

"The reading of the will."

"You've been invited to that?"

Smite smiled at them. "Yeah. Weird, right?"

"Indeed," said Freeman.

61

Snoot and Loblolly both took a step back when Art Travis Tee walked up to them by the fermentation tank where Fontaine had met his end. They had heard he was a big man, but had not expected him to be this big, and with that black hair and beard, there was only one way to describe the look he gave them: menacing.

"What now?" said Tee. "I thought you guys were done with me?" He looked at all the fresh crime-scene tape. "And what's this all about?"

Snoot stepped forward and offered her hand, surprised at the weakness of the handshake. "Just double-checking a few things—here and with you."

"Like what?"

Loblolly stepped forward and shook his hand, and immediately gave Snoot a look that seem to say, yes, he's a big one, but gentle. "I'm Detective Loblolly, Art. We just wanted to run a timeline by you and see what you have to say?"

Tee shrugged. "Whatever."

"Okay," said Snoot. "We've sort of spliced together the CCTV camera footage to come up with a timeline for the murder."

"Okay."

"We have you entering this area at 6:23 p.m. on the evening of the murder."

"Is that so?"

"Yes," said Loblolly. "And when you arrived here, there were three other people: McBride, Fontaine, and a man called Harry Smite."

"The protestor guy."

"Yes," said Snoot. "Do you remember seeing them?"

"Yes, Fontaine was yelling at that Smite guy, telling him to get the hell out of our winery."

"Right," said Loblolly. "We have you leaving the area at 6:25 p.m. What else happened while you were there?"

"Not much. I wanted to ask Fontaine about a tweak to the formula for Duct Tape Chardonnay, but I guess my timing was bad."

"Bad?" said Snoot.

"Yeah, he turned on me, as usual, saying there would be no changes now or ever. In fact, I think those were his exact words."

"And how did you respond?" said Loblolly.

Tee rubbed a hand through his beard. "Look, me and Mr. Fontaine never got along. Had almost come to blows a couple of times."

"Blows? When?"

Tee waved her off. "Doesn't matter. Plenty of times. The thing is, I have a terrible temper, too, so I thought it best to just turn on my heels and leave him alone."

"So you left?" said Snoot.

"Quickly."

"To calm down?" said Loblolly.

"Yes."

"Then why did you come back ten minutes later, at 6:33 p.m.?"

Tee averted his eyes. "Um."

"We have you there again from 6:33 p.m. to 6:34."

Tee ran a hand through his hair. "Let me think, let me think. Oh, yes. Blanche—I mean Ms. LaTour—asked if I had seen Mr. Fontaine, and I thought it would be easier to just take her where I had last seen him. You know, than just tell her."

"You really wanted to run into Fontaine, again?" said Snoot.

Tee shrugged. "Not really, but I wanted to be respectful to Ms. LaTour. And he was usually much calmer in her presence."

"Did she say why she was looking for Mr. Fontaine?" said Loblolly.

"No."

"Did she look upset or angry?"

Tee pursed his lips, considering the question. "She's hard to read most of the time. Pretty much has a sour look all the time, so I guess she could have been angry, but I sure couldn't swear to it."

"Okay," said Snoot. "So did you see Fontaine again?"

"No, he wasn't here when I came back with Ms. LaTour. Only McBride."

"Did you talk to him?" said Loblolly.

"No."

"Not a word?" said Snoot.

"No."

"For a full minute?" said Loblolly.

Tee shrugged. "I'm a quiet man."

"What about McBride and LaTour?" said Snoot. "Did they say anything?"

Tee chuckled.

"What's so funny?" said Soot.

"LaTour is a whisperer. If she wants to talk to you about something, she usually pulls you aside and whispers, so no one else can hear what she's saying."

"That's odd," said Loblolly.

"That's her," said Tee. "Anyway, she pulled McBride aside and talked to him."

"But you couldn't hear them?" said Snoot.

Tee shook his head.

"Did she or he seem upset?" said Loblolly.

"Not at all. She whispered and he nodded. She whispered again and he nodded again. And that's pretty much all."

"Pretty much?" said Snoot.

"No, actually, that was it."

"And then you left, quickly," said Loblolly.

"Yes, I had an experiment in progress back in my lab, so I wanted to get back to it as quickly as I could."

Snoot caught sight of Jeremy Polk and Captain Morgan arriving at the scene. "Mr. Tee, thank you for your help. We'll get back to you again if need be."

Tee nodded at both of them. "Okay, enjoy your day."

Loblolly and Snoot watched him amble away.

Snoot whistled softly through her teeth. "That's one big man."

62

The difference between the two vineyards couldn't have been more striking. The Château de Crabbe Rouge was an industrial factory, all business and stainless steel. The Château du Nez Bleu by contrast was everything you expected from a vineyard, from its stately main house, which looked like it had been plucked from the French countryside, to the line after line of grape vines surrounding the house, to the outbuildings surrounded by used and new oak barrels, to the main vineyard building, a large barn where the business of harvesting, fermenting, and bottling took place.

Sebastian Smythe, owner of the Château du Nez Bleu, also looked the part, from his grape-stained trousers, to his gray apron, to his wide-brimmed Panama hat. He was older than Fontaine by about ten years, his face bronzed and wrinkled from too many hours in the sun. A gray goatee and a matching ponytail completed the image of a man who relished his job, who wasn't content to sit behind a desk, who had to be out there, every day, tending to the grapes and coaxing them through the process to wine.

Grave and Freeman now sat opposite him, on either side of a long, rough-hewed table tucked beneath the branches of a tall white oak. The table itself was draped with a red and white checkerboard cloth and topped by a tray of cheese and fruit and bread and a selection of the estate's wines. Smythe had pulled a single grape from a bunch and was twirling it in his fingers, admiring its color.

"Help yourselves, gentlemen," said Smythe.

Grave held up a hand. "Perhaps later. First we have a few questions."

"Let me guess—Falcon Fontaine."

"Indeed," said Grave. "First, if you don't mind, please tell us about the transaction you and Mr. Fontaine were considering."

Smythe shrugged. "I couldn't believe it when he first proposed it. I was to get forty percent of his vineyard in exchange for $700,000."

"That's a lot of money," said Freeman.

"Indeed, it is, but to get forty percent ownership of your major competitor would have been worth every penny of it. Plus, it would have made us both more efficient. He could concentrate on Duct Tape Chardonnay and I could focus on my award-winning Blue Nose Pinot Noir. It's quite exceptional, you know." He picked up a bottle. "Here, may I pour you a glass?"

Grave shook his head. "On duty, I'm afraid."

Smythe sat the bottle back down. "Pity."

"As I understand it," said Grave, "he was going to use the money to build a vineyard on Mars."

Smythe chuckled. "Sounds ridiculous, doesn't it? But his wine—if you want to call it that—was a perfect match for the task. It's just chemicals. Nature need not apply."

"So you were going to go through with the deal?" said Freeman.

"Oh, absolutely, but the man was murdered before we could put pen to paper."

Grave nodded. "As I understand it, you arrived with Dilby, the lawyer, at about 6:45."

"Yes, lawyer and legal documents at the ready, but no Fontaine."

"And you left about seven minutes later."

Smythe cocked his head. "That sounds about right, and I was angry, very angry. We had a deal, dammit."

Smythe squished the grape and threw it to the ground. "A *deal*."

"And now?" said Grave.

Smythe looked confused. "Now? What do you mean?"

"Fontaine is dead. What happens to his vineyard now?"

"Oh, oh, I see what you mean. Well, from my point of view, I'll have to wait until the family decides what they want to do. I've long wanted to buy them out."

"And you discussed this with Mr. Fontaine?"

Smythe laughed. "Oh, my goodness, no. Fontaine would never have sold the whole vineyard. No, I had a few casual conversations with Frankie Fontaine, who's the logical successor, and with Fontaine's daughter, Lola, when she returned from France. A beautiful woman, don't you think?"

Grave could feel a British accent coming on, as well as the urge to jab his finger into Mr. Smythe's chest.

63

Captain Morgan greeted Snoot and Loblolly and then turned to Polk. "You know what to do?"

"Of course," said Polk, and then he began walking away from the crime scene.

"Where's he going?" said Snoot.

"A detail, one that may be important in the long run."

"What kind of detail?" said Loblolly.

"Just a detail," he said. "Now, as to the emergency doors . . ."

"Right," said Snoot. "We've sealed off the area again, as you can see, so the forensics folks should be able to get some prints, if there are any."

"Good," said Morgan.

"So," said Loblolly, "was Smithers-Watson able to see anything from the outside CCTV cameras?"

Morgan motioned both of them forward and whispered. "Yes, another detail, but I don't want to discuss it here. Back at the station, okay."

"Yes, sir."

Morgan looked toward the ceiling. "Where are your drones?"

"Outside," said Snoot.

"All right, do me a favor. Call the rest of the team and have them meet us back at the station in exactly an hour."

"But we still have others to interview," said Loblolly.

"I think you'll find that's not necessary, and if it is, we can do that after the reading of the will tomorrow morning."

"Whatever you say, sir," said Snoot. She turned to Loblolly and motioned her away from Morgan. "Come on, Polly, let's see what our flying critters are up to."

Loblolly and Snoot waved goodbye and walked quickly to the door and out into the fresh air. Sparky and Midnight were soon hovering in front of them, ready to make calls.

64

They went around the table twice, first to reveal any new information, and second to discuss and analyze all they knew—or didn't know—about the case.

Morgan turned to Charlize. "I think you said it best, Charlize. It's complicated."

"Indeed, it is, sir," said Charlize. "A good case can be made against several of them, either individually or as a group. Opportunity, motive, it's all there for anyone and everyone to see."

Morgan turned to Grave. "You're the lead on this. What do you think?"

Grave looked at his watch. "I think Charlize is right, and if the information I'm expecting back from Polk is what I think it's going to be, I think we'll have our killer—or one of them."

"You mean what Smithers-Watson saw on the SyncVision?"

"Well, no, but that, too." He turned to Smithers-Watson. "That was a brilliant catch."

"Then what?" said Morgan.

"Just a hunch. I asked Polk to do some checking for me, about the poison in Fontaine's system."

"The what-do-you-call-it."

"Yes, the Thycrabadol."

"But that didn't kill him, Grave."

"No, but it was intended to. It's where this mystery began. The poison and the reason for the poisoning."

Morgan was about to say something about motive, but the door to the conference room swung open, and Jeremy Polk walked in. He got straight to the point. "Grave, I got what you asked."

"And?" said Grave.

"It's complicated."

65

Grave pulled into his reserved space at his lighthouse home and turned off the Sprite, the roar of gospel music replaced by the crash of waves on the rocks that surrounded the lighthouse's base.

It was after dark, and all the lights in the lighthouse were on except for the lighthouse beam, which had been retired years ago, making the way for Grave to purchase the lighthouse. He climbed out of the car and headed into the tower. His scientist friend Red, the simcrab, was sitting silent on the first floor, plugged into his charging station, so Grave just headed up the circular steps to the kitchen level. Even before he reached the kitchen, he could tell from the movie soundtrack that his manservant, Roderick, was immersed in another Surround Vision showing of *Casablanca*.

Grave thought to rouse him and request dinner, but food was the farthest thing from his thoughts. Roderick must have sensed that because a bottle of chilled Duct Tape Chardonnay was waiting on the kitchen counter. Grave poured himself a glass and began the climb to the bedroom level, where he could hear soft whispering.

The scene he came upon startled him a little. His father, Jacob, was in bed, his fiancé, Ida Notion, in a small chair at the side of the bed, holding his hand.

"What happened?" said Grave.

Ida startled. "Oh, oh, there you are at last."

"Ida, what happened? Is he okay?"

"Yes, he's fine now. Choked on a bit of crab meat while cleaning his nails with that damned little knife of his. Gave us quite a scare. But he's resting now. Been asleep for about fifteen minutes."

Grave sighed with relief. "Great, but what are you guys doing here, anyway?"

Ida smiled at him. "You forgot completely, didn't you?"

Grave couldn't fathom what she was talking about.

"The wedding arrangements. Tonight was the night we were all going to sit down and settle on dates, flowers, the whole shebang."

Grave shook his head. "I'm so sorry. This case is consuming me. It's so complicated. Too many suspects."

"Did my vision help?"

"Yes, I think it's going to hold up in the end, but matching the right players has been a little difficult."

"You should put them all in the same room and grill them. Break them down."

Grave chuckled. *Like that would work*, he thought. And then he noticed the little knife on the nightstand next to Jacob.

66

Jacob Dilby called it his "closing suit," a sharkskin suit that flashed gray or blue depending on the light and sometimes seemed to strobe, making him look like some unknown force trying to materialize or dematerialize. It gave him confidence, and calmed him, all the while making him the center of attention.

He sat now at a small table brought in for the event, which the staff had positioned in front of four rows of five folding chairs each in the main lobby. Every seat was occupied. He recognized some of the staff, but not others. He wondered whether all these people were even mentioned in the will, or if they were just among the curious.

Blanche LaTour was standing at her chair, surveying the scene and counting the people in the other chairs. When she saw Harry Smite sitting in the back row, she frowned and shook her head. Then she turned to Dilby and nodded.

Time to begin.

Dilby pulled a sheaf of documents out of his briefcase, and placed his hands on top of them. "Ladies and gentlemen, if we may begin." He paused, waiting for the last murmurs of conversation to cease.

"I am here this morning to read the last will and testament of Mr. Falcon Pierre Fontaine, including a codicil completed by Mr. Fontaine and registered by me two days before his death."

He paused, noting the stirring of the people in their seats and a few mumbled words.

"Let us start with that codicil, because it informs us on the interpretation of the main document itself, and the disposition of Mr. Fontaine's estate."

He picked up the document and was about to begin reading, but the door to the main lobby burst open. Twenty Officer Larrys trotted in, followed by Captain Morgan and the entire Crab Cove Detective team.

Grave separated himself from the crowd and strode into the room and up to Dilby's table. "Before you do that, Mr. Dilby, I have a few words to say to this group."

67

Grave waited until the Officer Larrys, Captain Morgan, Jeremy Polk, and the other detectives moved into position around the rows of people. If anyone tried to make a run for it, their run would be brief and their arrest swift.

Grave paused briefly to look into the faces of the suspects. Lola LaFarge looked annoyed. Her brother looked at his watch and shook his head. Blanche LaTour looked away, as did Angus McBride and Art Travis Tee. Nigel Forthwith III, who wasn't a suspect at all, managed to look more nervous than any of the others. George Gitt, the head of security, crossed his arms and stared back. Harry Smite smiled at him and waved as if this was the most fun he'd had in a long time. Many others just waited patiently for him to begin.

Grave took a deep, calming breath. *I just need to lay out the facts*, he thought. *Without an accent. Without jabbing my finger.*

He looked back at Dilby, who gave him a nod, urging him to proceed.

Grave cleared his throat and then turned to the crowd.

"The person who killed Falcon Pierre Fontaine is in this room." He paused for effect, but the effect was minimal: a few head shakes, a few shrugs, a few people looking around the room, but no show of alarm from anyone.

"We need only look at the facts, and all becomes clear. I only ask that, as we proceed with the laying out of those facts, that you reserve question and comment. Then I'd be happy to deal with your reactions, whatever they may be."

He looked around the crowd. No one seemed to have an objection. "Good. Let's start with Mr. Fontaine himself. From our interviews with you, we know that he was not well liked. In fact, there are no fewer than eight of you who had good reason to strike him down."

He paused and looked around the room. "But only one of you did." He thought he detected a few suppressed smiles, particularly from Blanche LaTour. And others, including McBride, seemed to be stifling an impulse to look around. He definitely had their attention.

He raised his voice. "At precisely 6:22 p.m. on the evening of the murder, Falcon Fontaine entered an area that should have been covered by a CCTV camera, but wasn't. He didn't leave that area until the next morning, when his body was discovered floating in the fermentation tank also covered by that defunct camera.

"The murderer thought himself—or *her*self—clever in that regard. With the camera out of action, no one would see the crime. Which brings me to my first point of fact and my first question. Fact, the murder was planned. This was no spur-of-the-moment crime of passion. No, every detail was worked out, perhaps even practiced."

He paused. All eyes were on him. Good.

"And so we come now to our first question, the beginning of the unraveling. Who knew the camera covering the murder scene would be out of operation on that day, at that time? Well, George Gitt would have known . . ."

Gitt startled and jumped to his feet. "I didn't kill him. Don't you dare say I did."

Grave nodded. "I am saying nothing . . . at this point."

He motioned Gitt back into his seat. "Please, sit down. Now, Gitt knew and the repairman knew, and Angus McBride knew."

Now it was time for McBride to leap to his feet. "I'm the maintenance engineer. Of course I'd know. What does that prove? I mean all the maintenance schedules are on clipboards outside my office. Anyone could have seen them."

Grave motioned McBride back into his seat. "Of course, but please sit down, sir. We will know soon enough who not only knew about the schedule, but acted on it."

He pointed over the crowd. "Back there, behind the fermentation tank, is an emergency exit. Another example of planning. It's covered with the fingerprints of several people sitting in this room. And there's still more. A CCTV tape showing a limousine pulling up outside that door several days ago, long before the murder. Planning, you see. Should the emergency exit be the escape exit? Or does the presence of active CCTV cameras rule that out?"

Grave started to raise a finger, but thought better of it. "The latter is the answer. Too risky. So the murderer came through the front door of this winery, walked to the scene of the crime, and murdered Falcon Pierre Fontaine."

He paused. "But then a strange miracle happened. The murderer fled, but somehow the dead Fontaine managed to throw himself into the fermentation tank without leaving blood behind him on the floor."

Grave turned to Smithers-Watson. "Some of you have already met Detective Smithers-Watson. In reviewing the CCTV footage, he came upon something interesting. Something that can help us understand how Fontaine got into that tank without leaving blood behind."

He motioned for Smithers-Watson to step forward.

"We reviewed all the available CCTV tapes," said Smithers-Watson, "and we were able to identify every person who entered or left the area of the fermentation tank at or near the time of the murder. Some of you, many of you, moved into and out of that area during that timeframe. But there was something else, too. There were two robovacs that moved into and out of the area during that time."

"Exactly," said Grave. "And what do you think we found inside those robovacs?" He raised an eyebrow. "Blood. Falcon Pierre Fontaine's blood."

He cocked his head. "Someone cleaned up after the murderer. A friend, perhaps, or someone who hated Fontaine as much as the murderer. So now we have a *conspiracy* to commit murder. But how many people are involved? The CCTV footage indicates that eight people moved into and through that area within minutes of the time of death."

He paused again and scanned the people sitting in front of him. "And those eight people are sitting here now, hoping for some kind of inheritance. But who among them was involved in the planning and execution of the murder?"

He turned back to Dilby. "Thank you for your patience. It won't be long now." He turned back to the crowd. "There's an important fact that not many of you know. Or two, actually. First, Mr. Fontaine had cancer and was only months away from death when he was murdered. Second, someone was actively poisoning him at the time of his death. Just a few more days, and he would have been dead. So why stab him to death?"

He shook his head. "Perhaps we have a murderer and a would-be murderer. Two people acting independently, or perhaps in concert."

There were several gasps from the crowd, but Grave couldn't tell who had done the gasping. "Dr. Jeremy Polk, are you here?"

Polk stepped out from behind two Officer Larrys.

"Doctor, please tell these good folks about that poison."

Polk arched his back and strained his neck, trying to make himself appear taller. "The poison in question is Thycrabadol. Colorless, odorless, tasteless, and very difficult to detect postmortem. But as difficult as it is to detect in the human body, it is easy to detect in or on anything it touches."

He pulled out a teacup from a small black bag. "Take this teacup. Mr. Fontaine's very own. And filled time and time again by the person closest to him." He turned and pointed at Blanche LaTour. "His secretary."

Blanche LaTour made an attempt to run, but two Officer Larrys forced her back down in her chair and cuffed her.

"Blanche LaTour," said Grave. "You are under arrest for attempted murder and conspiracy to commit murder."

Grave began pacing back and forth in front of them. "Now, let's get back to the murder, which was an exercise in greed and revenge. And yes, there was one murderer, one person who stabbed Mr. Fontaine, but that person was assisted by others.

"The perpetrators were clever in selecting an area of the winery not covered by a camera. No one could see what they did."

He smiled and continued pacing. "But what about hearing? What if someone heard the last cries of Falcon Pierre Fontaine?"

Grave looked down at Lola. She was smirking and shaking her head. "Do you think that impossible, Lola?"

"I think it ridiculous." She almost spat the words out.

"So consider this." He paused and looked up at the ceiling. "Perhaps no one was there to hear it. Perhaps it is, as Ms. LaFarge says, ridiculous to even consider that. On the other hand, perhaps some *thing* heard it."

He pointed at the ceiling and shouted, "Felix!"

A deep, low voice answered. "Yes?"

"Who killed Falcon Pierre Fontaine?"

Lola jumped from her seat and bolted for the door. She made it only a few steps before she was scooped up by Bacchus. "Not so fast, missy."

Two Officer Larrys cuffed her and forced her back into her seat.

"Lola LaFarge," said Grave, "I arrest you for the murder of your father." He swept his hand across the crowd. "Officer Larrys, to your positions."

Officer Larrys moved quickly, taking Frankie Fontaine, Angus McBride, and Art Travis Tee into custody.

"You are all under arrest, for murder and conspiracy to commit murder. Gentlemen, take them all away, except for Ms. LaFarge."

Officer Larrys led the others out of the building.

Grave walked up and looked down at Lola. "You've cut my story short. I hadn't even gotten to the part where I ask you to empty the contents of your purse on Dilby's table here, to reveal your little every-day-carry knife, the one you used to clean your nails when we were, um, *involved*."

She turned away from him, saying nothing.

He turned to Dilby. "Sorry for the interruption. You may now proceed."

Grave turned and began moving toward the door, along with the rest of the team and the Officer Larrys escorting LaFarge out. Behind him, he could hear Dilby laying out the terms of inheritance.

Once outside, Captain Morgan was the first to congratulate him.

"That was something, Grave. Really something."

"Thank you, sir. A real team effort."

"But one thing, if I may ask."

"Sir?"

"Why the French accent?"

Epilogue

Detective Snoot took a sip of coffee and smiled across the table at Detective Loblolly, who was finishing a bite of a Little Willy Cruller, Skunk 'n Donuts' signature donut. "That was something, really something."

Polly nodded. "The will, you mean?"

"Well, that too, but no, the way Grave handled himself back there."

"Except for the French accent."

Amanda scoffed. "Accent schmaccent, he was great."

Polly smiled. "He was, wasn't he?"

"Indeed, he was."

"But you have to be happy for your lover boy, Harry Smite."

Amanda beamed. "Incredible. When that Dilby guy read the will, I was gobsmacked."

"Me, too. Glad we stayed behind."

"That was some codicil. How did it go? Anyone who may have taken part in my murder is hereby eliminated from my will?"

"Something like that. And when they read out your lover boy's name as sole beneficiary of the estate, I just about peed my pants."

Amanda chuckled. "I hope no one heard my little yelp."

Polly rolled her eyes. "Like everyone, is all."

"Talk about revenge," said Amanda.

"Yeah, so, when are you going to make your move on him?"

Amanda frowned. "Not. I mean, he's cute—and wealthy—but I don't know. No telling how these new riches will affect him. Yeah, no, I'm going to wait and see on that one." She looked over Polly's shoulder. Polly's drone, Sparky, was racing up to them. "Here, what's this?"

"Detective," said Sparky. "Captain Morgan wants you down at Le Crabe Bleu stat."

"What's up?"

"He just said there was an incident that needs your attention. Freeman will give you the details when you get there."

"Okay," said Amanda, "let's go."

"Not you," said Sparky. "Morgan wants you back at the station. Wants you to take the lead on getting statements from McBride and Tee."

Amanda groaned. "What fun."

• • •

Victoria Skunkford smiled up at Grave. "What a wonderful story."

"Except for the French accent part."

"No, I like that, too."

"Well, you may be the only one."

"No, don't be silly. Anyway, you should know that Falcon Fontaine is almost giddy about the reading of the will."

"He heard about that already?"

"Oh, no, he was there. We gave him a pass, hoping a little field trip would set him right, accept his fate, and all of that."

"And?"

"I hate to say it, but in his case, revenge was sweet. He is a changed man. Very cooperative, breezing through orientation, talking about the future."

"Wow."

"Indeed."

Grave spotted his drone, Barry, flying up the path toward them. "Here, what's this?"

"Emergency, sir," said Barry. "Morgan wants you down at Le Crabe Bleu immediately. Some sort of incident. Freeman is already there."

Grave sighed. "Sorry to leave you."

"Leave me?" said Barry. "No, I'm coming with you."

"No, I was talking to Victoria."

Barry groaned. "Your imaginary ghost friend?"

"She's not—well, forget about that. Let's get going." He stood and started walking back to the Sprite, then turned back to Victoria. "See you soon. Take care."

"You, too," said Victoria. "You, too."

•   •   •

Ten minutes later, Grave pulled into the parking lot of Le Crabe Bleu and climbed out of the Sprite. A gauntlet of Officer Larrys directed him into the restaurant and up to their banquet room, where a single candle-lit table sat in the center of the vast space. Polly was sitting there looking beautiful, but the look on her face suggested she was far from pleased to be there.

A voice from behind him startled Grave. "Take a seat, sir."

Grave spun around to see Detective Freeman and not Detective Freeman. He was dressed all in white. "Oh, no, you're not—"

"God? Well, of course I am. And you know what, I may just stay God from now on. Just look at these threads."

"Very nice." He looked over at Polly. "So what's this?"

"Why, a special dinner, of course, for you and Miss Polly."

"But—"

"No objections." He grabbed Grave by the hand and dragged him over to the table. "Miss Polly, your dinner date has arrived."

Polly crossed her arms. "I told you—"

"Shush," said God. He turned to Simon. "Sit down. Now."

Simon sat down.

"Now, perhaps God is wrong about this, but God doesn't think so. Enjoy this dinner. Talk. Come to an understanding. Or not. What I'm providing here is opportunity, away from the distractions of work."

Simon said nothing.

Polly said nothing.

God nodded. "Okay, silence is at least a start. Now, when I leave, begin talking. About anything. Including me. God."

He smiled at them, bowed, and began walking away. As he reached the exit, he turned and called back to them. "And remember, *What therefore God hath joined together, let not man put asunder.*"

And then he was gone.

Simon looked at Polly.

Polly looked at Simon.

Both looked away.

Simon cleared his throat and looked at her again. "Do you think the French accent was too much?"

She burst out laughing. "No, Simon, it was just right."

They talked well into the evening.

The Universe, which had been watching everything with great interest, smiled. But it was a sly smile—and complicated.

Note From The Author

Word-of-mouth is crucial for any author to succeed. If you enjoyed *Simon Grave and the Wrath of Grapes*, please leave a review online— anywhere you are able. Even if it's just a sentence or two. It would make all the difference and would be very much appreciated.

Thanks!
Len

About the Author

Len Boswell is the author of eleven additional books, including mysteries, fantasies, memoirs, and other nonfiction works. He lives in the mountains of West Virginia with his wife, Ruth, and their two dogs, Shadow and Cinder.

We hope you enjoyed reading this title from:

www.blackrosewriting.com

Subscribe to our mailing list – *The Rosevine* – and receive **FREE** books, daily deals, and stay current with news about upcoming releases and our hottest authors.
Scan the QR code below to sign up.

Already a subscriber? Please accept a sincere thank you for being a fan of Black Rose Writing authors.

View other Black Rose Writing titles at
www.blackrosewriting.com/books and use promo code
PRINT to receive a **20% discount** when purchasing.

Lightning Source UK Ltd.
Milton Keynes UK
UKHW041129060323
418104UK00001B/1